Nightmare at Norton's Mills

Other Apple Paperbacks
you will enjoy:

Trouble at Moosehead Lake
by James and Lois Cowan

Chocolate-Covered Ants
by Stephen Manes

Into the Dark
by Nicholas Wilde

Wizard's Hall
by Jane Yolen

The Adventures of Boone Barnaby
by Joe Cottonwood

Ghost in the Noonday Sun
by Sid Fleischman

Nightmare at Norton's Mills

James and Lois Cowan

AN
APPLE
PAPERBACK

SCHOLASTIC INC.
New York Toronto London Auckland Sydney

DISCLAIMER

The Emergency Rescue! series is meant to protect young readers from harm by teaching them to 1) recognize problems, then 2) seek professional help. The information in the five stories in this book must not substitute for medical advice and certified rescue training.

ISBN 0-590-46019-6

12 11 10 9 8 7 6 5 4 3 2   4 5 6 7 8/9

Printed in the U.S.A   40

First Scholastic printing, August 1993

Acknowledgments

The authors acknowledge the kind assistance and technical advice of Tammy Harrington, Lifeguard Training Instructor & W.S.I., National American Red Cross; Student Sarah McGinnis; Gary Gertloff, Central Maine Power; Gretchen Labbe, Wilderness Rescue Team; Nancy McGinnis, Children's Librarian, Bailey [Winthrop, Maine] Library; Rick Petrie, EMT-Paramedic, Life Safety Consultants of New England; the original Janey Waterpaws, SAR dog, Telluride, Colorado; Dottie Morales, Librarian, Camden [Maine] Public Library; Virginia Hall, RN, EMT-Intermediate; Kenneth Bailey, Camden [Maine] Lake Warden; Lieutenant Richard Morse, Safety Officer, Maine Forest Service; Karl & Linda Drechsler, Hope [Maine] Orchards; Shawn Walsh, University of Maine Hockey Coach; James Kilgour, MD, FACEP; Jim Morrissey, WEMT-Paramedic, Vice President, Wilderness Medical Associates; Kevin McGinnis, EMT-Paramedic, Director, Maine EMS; and Lieutenant Carter Smith, Maine Warden Service.

Dedicated to
Davey Cowan, the kid;
Davey Rich, forever the kid;
and all those other Daveys out there.

Contents

Decoder Guide

Ten-01	unable to copy	**Ten-32**	person with weapon
Ten-02	receiving well	**Ten-36**	What time is it?
Ten-03	go ahead	**Ten-55**	vehicle accident
Ten-04	OK	**Ten-56**	send a wrecker
Ten-06	I'm busy	**Ten-60**	lost person
Ten-07	out of service	**Ten-61**	hunting accident
Ten-08	I'm available	**Ten-62**	drowning
Ten-09	repeat, please	**Ten-65**	boating accident
Ten-10	out of vehicle	**Ten-66**	snowmobile accident
Ten-13	weather	**Ten-71**	bomb threat
Ten-19	go to station	**Ten-72**	fire alarm
Ten-20	give your location	**Ten-79**	plane crash
Ten-21	call by telephone	**Ten-81**	smoke
Ten-23	stand by	**Ten-91**	call your home

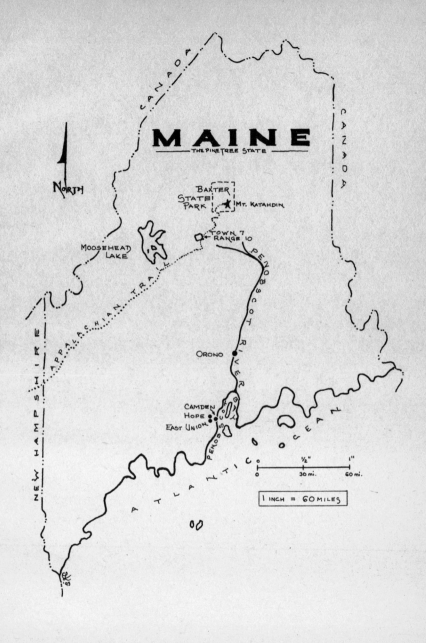

1
Cramp

The muscles in his left thigh vibrated like steel guitar strings, cranked to the limit.

And there was the pressure.

His thigh felt like it was no longer part of him. If he'd been asked, Michael Douglas Knight — nicknamed Mid for his first two initials — would have said that his leg belonged to someone else.

But there wasn't anyone there who was going to ask. The cramp had caught him in the middle of the pond, far from shore.

Mid was alone.

Oh sure, his kid brother, Jason, those two Camden kids Davey and Matt, and some local dweebs were in the pond, too, horsing around, playing Marco Polo.

But there was no one he could *count* on.

The problem with his thigh — and the pain — were his.

But hey, he was tough. Mid, the college athlete, was used to injuries, had disciplined himself to play through them. Got a bad bruise on the back of your thigh? Loosen it up and skate anyway.

Yeah, Mid knew all about pain . . . could take it on the chops.

But this was different.

The dead weight of Mid's numb thigh was an anchor. It was about to drag him down to the bottom of Norton's Mills Pond.

Mid was going to drown.

The thought started him trembling.

He buried his head in the chilly water to grab his leg. He rubbed. The pain sharpened, and he gasped. Water poured into his mouth.

He gagged.

Mid's thrashing arms brought him back to the surface. Through a blur of water, he could hear his brother Jason playing and laughing.

Mid was six years older than Jason. Their folks had never bothered to ask, but Mid hadn't been thrilled with the prospect of a kid brother, somebody else for Dad to play catch with.

Of course, Baby Jason always dropped the ball. He was not the jock his big brother was.

Jason didn't know about playing through pain.

Mid had never imagined that someday he might have to count on his wimp brother. But no way was

2

Mid going to make it to shore on his own.

He'd be doin' good if he could keep his head above water long enough for Jason and his pals to do something.

Anything.

"*Helllp!* Jason! Hey, Jase, I need help!"

* * *

Earlier that morning as Davey Mountain was scurrying around his house in Camden, Maine, a near-drowning at Norton's Mills was not a piece of his plans for the day.

He and his cousin Matt Rich were going swimming out at Jason Knight's.

Matt had just biked over to the Mountains' House. "Hey Aunt Jill, . . ." Matt grinned at Davey's mom as he stepped through her front door, "it's ten o'clock. Ready to roll?" Davey's mom was driving the two boys to Jason's in East Union, just over the Hope town line.

Mrs. Mountain and Matt shared a smile. They both knew that Davey was frequently late. "I'll be in the office with Dad," she called to Davey in the next room as she winked at Matt, "so yell when you want to go."

In the kitchen, Davey nodded as he grabbed his sweats and a damp red towel out of the dryer.

Then he began building a bag lunch, starting with a Toblerone chocolate bar from his freezer stash. Heavy-duty energy.

In front of the foyer mirror, Matt checked out a zit peeking from under his blond hair. Then, twirling his thumbs, he studied for the hundredth time the acrylic painting next to the mirror. An artist's conception of a baseball game in a neighborhood lot. The shadowing was terrific.

"Yo, Davey." Matt watched his own bulky body walk past the mirror toward the kitchen. "Let's rock 'n' roll. I've got enough food for a potluck suppah." Matt's Maine roots crept into his words.

He held up a French & Brawn grocery bag, folded three times at the top. His hand supported the bottom. "There's plenty for Jason, too," added Matt. "As usual."

Jason, Matt, and Davey had gotten to know each other sharing food and cheers for the University of Maine hockey team. Jason's family had season tickets next to the Mountains' seats at the arena up in Orono.

Jason's brother was Black Bear defenseman Mid Knight.

All winter long, in between mouthfuls of popcorn and hot dogs and penalty calls, Jason had talked about what a great time they'd all have next summer at Norton's Mills Pond with the East Union kids.

Matt and Davey had a standing invitation for the first warm day of the year.

This was it. Finally.

Matt stopped short at the kitchen door. Davey and his bulldog were in a tug-of-war over Davey's towel. The dog saw red like a bull.

The mutt was winning.

4

Through the kitchen window, a cloudless, windless day awaited the boys. The quiet harbor spread out in front of the Mountains' home, a converted boathouse. Camden's windjammer fleet was out cruising the Penobscot Bay islands, motor-sailing.

The water was dead calm. A swimming day, but in a lake. Maine's piece of the Atlantic Ocean was c-o-l-d.

I can't wait, Davey thought, as he ripped the towel through the bulldog's phony snarls, *to get to that pond.*

Davey missed a little hunk of red that Bossy kept as a trophy.

And he didn't foresee that, before the weather-perfect day was done, they'd have a situation, a Ten-62. A water emergency.

What was on Davey's mind, less than thirty minutes after he and Matt had piled into the Mountain family car, was the awesome day and how great summer felt.

Particularly when the car's top was down.

Mrs. Mountain turned off onto Old Route Seventeen. The red Saab convertible rolled by the Pioneer Grange Hall.

Matt, basking in the back with Davey, pointed to a street sign, then another. Throughout East Union, street names were carved into the sides of wooden birdhouses, long like covered bridges.

Davey peered, hawklike. Any bluebirds?

In the front, Bossy, riding shotgun, sampled the

5

air above his square head. Sniff. Fresh water, frogs, fish.

Ahead, a pond spread out from both sides of the road.

At the low bridge and before the Grace Fellowship building was a hinged sign: GRIST MILL AND COUNTRY STORE. There was a carved and painted likeness of Norton's Mills' 200-year-old shingled buildings on the sign, with the picture-perfect millpond in front.

What the sign left out was the neat diving board and an overhanging Tarzan rope.

And neighborhood kids — splashing, yelping, belly-flopping.

Catty-corner to the pond was the Knights' house. Off the side of the house, an ell connected white house to red barn. A hundred years ago, Great-grandfather Knight walked from his kitchen to his hayloft without having to shovel new-fallen snow or brave sub-zero temperatures.

Now the barn section was a garage, and the ell between the barn and the house was a skylit greenhouse.

The Mountains' jaunty convertible turned into the Knights' driveway and came to a halt alongside the Maine-style farmhouse, with its green shutters and doors.

The Saab sighed.

As the boys hopped out of the car — "No, no, Bossy, you can't go with them" — Davey's mom, grabbing the bulldog's scruff, said, "Now, guys, remember, I'm on duty 'til seven tonight. When you want to get picked up, I might be out on a run."

Mrs. Mountain, with her husband, was a writer. She also was on call this afternoon as a volunteer emergency medical technician with the Puckerbrush Rescue Squad.

As she plopped Bossy back down on the seat, she adjusted the EMT radio she wore on her hip. Whenever it bleeped, "Portable-40, Portable-40. . . . Ten-19 to the station," she would punch the transmit button to let her dispatcher know she was on her way: "Portable-40 to Puckerbrush. . . . I'll be Ten-08."

Mr. Mountain, Davey's father, was a volunteer firefighter with Camden's Puckerbrush Rescue. And Davey and Matt were both junior members of the squad. The cousins got involved in whatever training they could — medical emergencies, rescue attempts, extrication problems, firefighter responses.

But not today. The boys were in another town, in a different service area, hanging with a hockey-loving friend and his pals.

* * *

"Watch out! The rope's comin'!" Matt, hip-deep in the pond, yelled at his cousin.

Davey ducked.

On the end of the line, Alice, one of Jason's friends, flew over Davey's bent back. Her gangly legs thrashed.

The ride was out over the pond.

With a loud scream, Alice let go of the rope. Then stopped fooling around.

7

Her thin body took on the arched shape of a sword. Davey stopped his water-fight with Matt to watch.

She knifed into the pond and disappeared. Alice acting scared — and then turning out to be an expert diver. You have to be good at something, Davey realized, to fake being bad. Like clowns at rodeos or on a circus high wire.

The rope swung back toward Davey. He caught the knot, crawled out of the pond, and climbed the stairs to the Knights' back deck.

It was the first time he'd balanced himself atop the railing. There he was, teetering, with Matt, Jason, and other kids whose names he didn't know, all shouting, "Jump! Jump!"

He launched into space. Sailed out under the tree and then high above the pond.

At the instant before the rope started to swing back — frozen in the air — he bought it. "Geroni-moooo!"

Thunk! A human cannonball splash exploded the middle of the pond.

"Hey! Knock it off." On the deck above Matt's head towered Mid. "I'm trying to sleep," growled the not-so-jolly giant. "I was up working half the night. Ya know?"

Davey climbed up on the diving board, perched at the end, and eyed Mid. He'd seen Jason's brother, a sophmore defenseman, in action at plenty of UMaine hockey games. Not much of a goal scorer, but he sure liked to hit.

Turns out, Davey decided, The Mid's mean and tough off the ice, as well.

Davey watched Jason's eyes dart about checking out his friends' reaction to his older brother. It looked like Mid was gonna be a pain.

Davey broke the fragile silence. "Hey guys, I'm starved. How 'bout we go over next to the mill and eat?" *So the grumpy giant can get on with his beauty rest*, he thought.

But didn't say.

* * *

His lean belly full, Davey sat against the mill. He wrapped the leftover half of his Toblerone bar, saving the remaining Swiss chocolate for the afternoon. His tongue mined a gap between his teeth where a piece of almond had nose-dived.

On the pond, Matt bobbed in a life ring, scarfing down a handful of Nilla Wafers. His big tanned body spilled out over the ring's faded lettering: EVELYN C. — MONHEGAN.

"Quack. Quack."

A family of ducks followed behind.

"Quack."

Davey felt sluggish as he watched Alice doing lazy laps. *But she's some old fast*, he said to himself. His hawk eyes studied her smooth stroke. *Twenty-five, twenty-six, twenty-seven. . . . She's smokin'!*

Jason threw his bread crusts to the mallards and stood up. "Anyone for Marco Polo?"

Matt called out, "Last one in's a rotten egg."

With a group shout, everyone hit water.

They dog-paddled under the bridge to the other side of the road, behind the Knights', where it was deep.

The empty life ring bobbed in their wake.

* * *

"Marco," sang out Davey, his eyes squeezed tight. He was it. It drove him crazy to not be able to see what was going on.

"Polo." "Polo." From the other kids, all wide-eyed. "Polo."

Pause.

Davey strained his ears for clues. As he groped around in the water trying to tag someone, he would now-and-then call "Marco," then wait for sound-clues.

"Polo," all the kids in the game had to answer.

Davey heard someone dive under water.

"Marco," Davey called. Then listened.

"Polo. . . ."

"Polo."

Silence.

"Polo."

Aha. A voice was right over to his left. With a quick dive, Davey grabbed through the water. His hand closed on a piece of bathing suit.

When he opened his eyes, he found he'd gotten Alice.

Alice, now it, shut her eyes and waited for answers to her call.

10

"Polo. . . ."

"Polo."

She frowned at what sounded like about six kids kicking hard. She dropped straight down under the water, swam for about ten yards, surfaced and called out, "Marco."

"Polo. . . ."

"Polo."

"Polo."

With a lurch, she faked right.

Spun.

Leapt straight back.

Davey watched her grab at something. "Gotcha!"

She had Matt by his arm.

Just as Matt sighed, shut his eyes and said, "Marco," there was movement above him, on the Knights' deck.

It was The Mid. Flexing.

Davey pictured a bear leaving his cave.

Now Mid hiked up the waist of his swim trunks and filled his lungs. He dropped to the deck and snapped off a hundred push-ups.

Jason, bobbing near Davey, mumbled, "Why can't I have a nicer brother, like Jack the Ripper?"

"Marco."

"Polo."

"Polo."

The next time Davey thought to glance toward the house, Mid was gone. Davey looked around. At the far end of the pond, Mid was churning the water like an eggbeater.

Davey sighed. Mid was a pain, but what a jock.

"Polo."

"Polo."

"You're it, Jason!" Matt had tagged him. "Hasten, Jason, get the basin. Oops, slop! Get the mop!"

"Mar-co," Jason chimed out.

Davey dove under.

*　*　*

"*Helllp!* Jason! Hey, Jase, I need help!"

Was that Mid? Calling Jason? Davey, scurrying through the water, froze.

Matt spun toward the middle of the pond. "Was that The Mid?" he asked one of the East Union kids.

"Couldn't be."

Davey peered out into the middle of the pond. He watched Mid's head slip underwater.

Jason's friends stood in an uneasy circle near shore. Jason spaced out, froze, staring off somewhere.

"Portable-D." Matt got Davey's attention by using his Puckerbrush Rescue name.

Davey locked on his cousin's big tanned face.

"Looks like a possible Ten-62. Mid." Matt wiped the back of his hand across his mouth. "He's goin' under. In deep sneakers."

Matt's words unglued the others.

Alice turned to the biggest East Union kid. "Do something!"

12

"Whadaya mean, me?" He turned back on Alice. "You're the swimmer. Maybe you should go out there."

Jason worried his bottom lip with his front teeth. "Should we all go?" He wasn't sure.

"Whoa. No." Davey spoke. "Hold your horses. Nooo-body goes. I'll activate the nine-one-one system. *You* . . ." he eyeballed each one of them, ". . . listen to Matt."

"Find Sandy!" Jason shouted after Davey, who was stroking toward the bridge — and Norton's Mills' phone. "She runs things."

Sandy. There was an adult there, to help.

"Helllp. Damn it. I can't swim, I've got a. . . ." The rest of his words were lost underwater.

No one wanted to watch. Jason looked as if he were in pain.

Everyone turned to Matt.

"Let's consider the first thing," he said. "Is the scene safe, for us?"

"Hey," the big kid ignored Matt, "how 'bout all of us going out there and holding him up?"

"No. The scene's safe only as long as no one goes in after Mid." Matt stopped to think.

"The next thing to do is for everyone, us and Mid, to calm down." Matt turned toward the middle of the pond, cupped his hands around his mouth, and coached Mid in drownproofing. "Mid, float. Take a breath, put your head down, and float. Now rest. We've sent for help. And we'll get you out. Be cool and flloooaa-t. . . .

"When you need another breath, press your arms down to your sides and bring your legs together. Your head'll pop up. Grab another breath, then float again, with your head in the water."

Mid seemed to be trying to follow Matt's directions.

"Buuut . . ." one of the kids started.

Matt turned and faced them all. "Look, the last thing we do is go out there. He's in a panic. He'll pull us under. Rescuers can maybe deal with one person drowning, but seven? . . . Let's think. Can we reach him somehow from a safe place? No, he's too far out. Agreed? . . .

"So let's try the life ring."

* * *

Davey beat feet into the country store, dripping water and concern. Past shelf after shelf of wild blueberry waffle mix, coconut chips, kasha buckwheat. Dilly beans put up in mason jars.

Davey knew about all this stuff. Jason was a part-time stock boy here, filling shelves with spices, dried fruits. Labeling bags.

But where was this Sandy person? Davey stopped in front of the honey shelves and peered.

There was an old-timey circular dial phone on the counter.

He dialed 9-1-1.

Nothing.

9-1-1 didn't work.

What a nightmare, thought Davey. *What do I do now?*

14

Somewhere in the back of the building, a motor started. Davey crashed back, through storage and into what turned out to be the mixing room.

A woman with her hair in a bandanna was scooping sweet brown rice flour into a machine that looked like a push lawn mower.

"Sandy? We've got a drowning in progress. Need to call nine-one-one, activate EMS."

As they both moved toward the front part of the building, and the phone, he filled her in.

"The way we get Emergency Medical Services here," Sandy took wide strides, dusting flour off her arms and her COMMON GROUND FAIR apron, "is to dial a full number. . . ." She picked up the phone. 555-3540.

She handed Davey the phone, and galloped out the door toward the pond.

* * *

It had taken forever for one of the East Union boys to retrieve the life ring from the water on the other side of the road.

But it didn't much matter. Alice's best throw came up five yards short, and there was no way that Mid could swim to it.

He could barely surface for air.

"Great, Mid. You're doing great. . . ." There was a quiver in Jason's voice as he talked his brother down, as Matt had directed. "Now take a breath, then put your face in the water again. . . ." The drownproofing technique was still working.

Matt patted Jason on the shoulder and continued to monitor the rescue action.

Two kids had reached the other side of the pond and were flipping over a flat-bottomed rowboat.

Oars were stored underneath.

They slid the skiff off the grassy bank and into the pond.

They jumped in, sitting side by side.

Oars into oar locks.

Splash. Splash. Splash. In synch, they rowed toward Mid. *Splash. Splash. Splash.*

A group of kids waited by the pond edge for Matt. "Okay, now . . ." he said as he walked up.

"Great, Mid . . ." Jason called out from the knoll. "Now breathe. Keep it up . . . good. . . ."

"We'll form a chain," said Matt, "with Jason as the anchor on shore, so Mid can't pull us in." He turned to yell, "Jason!" and waved him over.

Jason jogged down to them.

"Grab onto that lowest branch," Matt directed, "and *don't let go.* The rest of us will lock arms in the water. We can get Alice out far enough so she can toss the ring to Mid. But he can't use the rope to drag her deeper 'cause she'll be linked to land by us." He nodded at the kids. "And," he turned to Jason, "by our anchor. You."

The boat was aiming toward Mid from the other side.

Twenty feet out from shore, Alice's left elbow linked through Matt's right arm. Her left hand held the coiled rope. The ring was in her other hand.

"Watch you don't bean him," Matt warned her, grasping the tail end of the line.

She focused on her target, squinted, then leaned back.

Her league-leading pitching arm whipped forward.

The ring arched out and down, splatting onto the water. Next to Mid.

"Perfecto," Matt whispered.

Mid threw hairy arms over the ring.

Then he hung there, gulping like a dog taking a pill.

"Careful!" cautioned Matt as the square stern of the skiff backed up to Mid.

The sound of a siren reached Davey's ears as he and Sandy watched the scene from the bridge. They saw Mid latch onto the boat.

Splash. Splash. Splash. The oars dipped in and out.

The boat slogged along with Mid dangling off the stern.

* * *

EMT Roger Atherton, who was also Norton's Mills' bookkeeper, checked out Mid while his partner took notes.

His medical survey completed, Roger rocked back on his heels, stroked his walrus mustache. "You seem fine, Mid. But you still need to get checked out in the emergency room.

"Probably that cramp was a muscle contraction,

you know, what folks call a charley horse. Something irritated your muscle fibers. They responded by tightening up. Maybe they ran out of oxygen?"

"A *charley horse*? No way, man." Mid pushed out his chest. "I've never felt anything like *that*. Yeah yeah, it's okay now, but you just don't know. . . ."

"Yeah, well." Roger continued to massage Mid's thigh as they talked. "Hey, you could have drowned. That's what happens. The pain is so intense, sometimes it overwhelms people. They forget to stay calm. You were lucky these kids were around."

Mid lowered his eyes.

* * *

Winter had come to Maine, and to Norton's Mills. The pond was thick with ice, and swooping tracks from kids' skates crisscrossed the surface.

Those same markings were being carved into the ice at Alfond Arena, where the Black Bear hockey team's Mid Knight was dishing out another superstar game.

One row behind the Maine bench, in the seats UMaine saved for VIPs, kids from Camden and East Union were nose-to-puck with the action as the Central Michigan forward broke out and streaked down the right wing.

The green-jersey'd forward cradled the puck on his stick, crossing the centerline and curving in toward the goal.

The Maine goalie drifted out of his net.

A breakaway.

Out of the blue, Mid raced back, angled the ice to pinch off the forward.

With a flash of skates in one motion he stopped, pivoted his hip, and nailed the attacker.

Arms, legs, stick, and skates went every which way as the green-shirt'd hockey player cartwheeled into the corner.

The puck drifted toward the Maine goalie.

This was the fourth crunching check that Mid had delivered. The Black Bears continued their lead, three to one.

"Didja see that? Did you see my brother cream that guy?" Jason jumped up. So did Matt. And Alice. All the kids were on their feet cheering The Mid.

"The green guys must be thinking that this is a bad dream," yelled Davey. "Every time they get set to do something . . . wham! The Mid comes out of nowhere and crunches 'em."

"Bad dream, huh," joined in Matt. "This isn't a bad dream, it's a Knight-mare!"

"Yeah. Knight-mare! Knight-mare!"

The chant worked down the row of kids.

"Knight-mare!"

Behind them a two-hundred-fifty-pound leather-lungs picked it up.

"KNIGHT-mare! KNIGHT-mare!!" The wooden rafters vibrated as a wave of voices joined in. "KNIGHT-MARE! KNIGHTMARE! KNIGHTMARE!"

Mid skated over to his team's bench.

As he swung his leg over the boards, he paused, caught Jason's eye. He gave his kid brother a thick hockey-gloved thumbs-up.

UMaine bowled over Central Michigan, 6–2.

Skill
Safe Water Rescue

WHAT is it? The way to help someone in trouble in water.

WHY do you do it? To save a life without losing your own.

WHEN do you do it? Whenever someone is at risk of drowning or thinks they are. Panic alone can lead to drowning. If a person lets you know they want help — even if you think they're kidding — assume it is an emergency. Activate the EMS system as Davey did, and then follow this procedure.

HOW do you do it? There are four steps to helping a drowning victim: **Reach → Throw → Row → Go**. 1) **Reach** from shore with your hand or foot. If the victim's too far out for that, extend your reach by holding out a pole, oar, fishing rod, or stick. Or throw out a rope, holding on to one end. STAY ON LAND, and guard against getting pulled into the water. 2) **Throw**. If the victim is too far out to reach, throw a ring buoy or a personal flotation device (PFD), a life jacket — anything that floats. Give the victim something to hold on to until more help arrives. 3) **Row**. Be careful to not hit the victim, and don't let the boat get tipped over by the panicked swimmer. 4) **Go**. If reaching, throwing, and rowing don't work or cannot be done (no boat, for example), only then is it time to consider going to the person. Take something with you that will help both you and your victim stay afloat. *Only trained, certified lifesavers should ever go.*

Is the scene safe?

Each step of Reach → Throw → Row → Go can save a life. So start with the safest — reaching — because it's the most likely to keep you out of trouble. Then throw, then row, and finally, as a last resort (if you are certified) go. The wetter you have to get, the more danger you are in. People afraid of drowning become superstrong and try to climb up on their rescuer's head, drowning their lifesaver (and themselves).

Don't be a dead hero.

* * *

To learn more about safe water rescue, read *Lifesaving* (Merit Badge Series), published by Boy Scouts of America, 1980.

Emergency Rescue! Report

Report number 6	My name MATT RICH

Incident location
OLD ROUTE 17
street
E. UNION,   MAINE
city/town   state

My address
BAY VIEW ST.
street
CAMDEN, ME   04843
city/town   state   zip

Was the scene safe?   yes   no   THE MID WAS IN TROUBLE
Describe the scene.   ☒   ☐   IN THE MIDDLE OF THE
MILLPOND. NO ONE WENT IN AFTER HIM. WE
FOLLOWED REACH → THROW → ROW → GO.

First name of victim MICHAEL	Age 21	male ☒	female ☐	**Aid first given by**

Aid first given by:
- ☒ me US
- ☐ someone else
- ☐ EMTs
- ☐ police
- ☐ firefighters

Transported to
REFUSED TRANSPORT

Describe any transportation or communication problems.
NO 9-1-1 PHONE NUMBER

Type of illness or injury or accident

- ☐ bone fracture
- ☐ aches and sprains
- ☐ bleeding injury
- ☐ illness
- ☐ fire
- ☐ auto or truck accident
- ☒ water incident
- ☐ HazMat
- ☐ airplane disaster
- ☐ lost person/search and rescue
- ☐ extrication
- ☐ animal incident
- ☐ electrical accident
- ☐ tornado
- ☐ hurricane
- ☐ blizzard
- ☐ other

Who called for help?

- ☐ me
- ☒ a friend DAVEY AND
- ☐ family member   SANDY
- ☐ professional responder
- ☐ neighbor
- ☐ other person

Emergency responders on the scene

- ☒ EMTs
- ☐ firefighters
- ☐ police
- ☐ HazMat
- ☐ emergency department
- ☐ utility crew
- ☐ search and rescue

Describe what happened, and the outcome. Include unusual circumstances. WE THREW A RING BUT IT DIDN'T
REACH. SO WE LINKED AND ALICE THREW AGAIN.
AT THE SAME TIME A BOAT STARTED OUT.
MID WAS TOWED IN!

my signature ___Matt Rich___

2
Charge

"Brrr." Davey, walking his dog, shivered inside his green-and-white rugby shirt.

October had arrived overnight, cold and gusty. Davey looked up as he walked by the big elm on his front lawn. He could see the tree's skeleton through its thinned leaves.

The bulldog sat on the Mountains' front stoop waiting for Davey to catch up.

"You want in, Boss?" Above the dog's head, Davey reached for the screen-door knob.

Fingers contacted cold metal.

"Ayyy!" Davey yelped as his hand needled with electrical shock. He flicked his fingers like a nurse shaking down a thermometer.

He tried the handle again, then unlatched the door.

Now that Bossy could go in, his hind quarters instead plopped onto the granite stoop. His Milk Dud eyes scanned from Davey's face to the doorway.

What to do? Where to be?

Then the dog caught sight of big Chancealong trotting toward the house with his master Matt Rich. "Woof," Bossy rumbled to the big chinook dog.

Two tails — one high, one low; one short, the other long — wagged. Two cousins nodded.

"Come *on*, Bossy," Davey prodded with his Bean boot. "*In*. You're gonna make Matt and me late for school."

As Chancy crowded the bulldog to get into the house, Bossy finally chose to move. His breakfast, waiting in a dish on the kitchen floor, was undefended.

Bulldog and chinook shouldered through the opening, the squat bulldog trotting beneath the butter-colored underbelly of the sled dog.

Davey shut the door against two moist brown noses.

Through the screen, Chancealong wore his You're-leaving-me-alone-*again*? expression, the one that reminded Matt of Chancy's mother, Jet Stream. Named for the Maine sailing breeze, the chinook was a thank-you to Matt who rescued Jet Stream after a Ten-55 — a truck rollover — up by Moosehead Lake.

Chancy and Bossy, who stuck together like peanut

butter and jelly, spent their days at the Mountains' whenever Matt's parents, Mr. and Mrs. Rich, were in Portland ordering supplies for Rich's Diner. The dogs would romp and then curl up on Bossy's beanbag. For human contact they could always pester Mr. and Mrs. Mountain, writing a book in their upstairs study.

"Make sure you shut the big door, boys." Dog ears perked at another voice inside the house.

The Mountains' heating system cut on for the first time since last winter.

* * *

Mr. Mountain's plea hadn't reached the cousins, already across the side lawn.

They loped alongside the mouth of the Megunticook River, where it poured into Penobscot Bay. The waterfall was running dark, fast, and cold.

Davey, shifting his backpack, gazed at the windjammers on moorings in the harbor. The fleet was sprouting its winter covers of wood and plastic.

Matt's Merrell hiking boots scattered a mound of new-fallen leaves as the boys rounded Ayer's Fish Market. The now-empty sidewalk lobster tank with its PLEASE DON'T FEED THE MALE OR FEMALE LOBSTERS sign was a reminder of summer tourists who would stand there, confused.

"Check the time, wouldja?" Matt asked Davey. "I think we're gonna be late."

Matt was never late.

Davey hooked a finger under the elastic wrist of his windshell. As he eagle-eyed his watch's analog face, a flash of pink almost bowled him over.

It was Louise Smith, a tornado of energy, black curls cascading over her pale rose sweater.

"Jeez, Louise." Davey steadied himself against the lobster tank. "Whereya going in such a rush? Matt's right here and school's the other direction."

Matt planted an elbow in Davey's ribs.

"Ooo, hi, Davey. Matthew. . . ." Math-YEW was the way Louise said it. ". . . I left my book report at home," she was panting through her smile. "Dad'll have to drive me to school if I'm gonna make homeroom. Did you finish yours, Matthew?"

Her apple cheeks glowed at him.

"See you in class, Matthew," she tossed his name over her shoulder as she moved into gear, up High Street and toward her family's Victorian bed-and-breakfast.

* * *

Minutes later, Matt and Davey were noodling up Washington Street, talking about Matt's book report on *Avalanche*. ". . . And then," said Matt, "this kid Chris decides to shoot this coyote, ya know. . . ."

"Hiiii, Matthew," sang out a pink flash from the passenger side of a Model-A pickup tooting by. Its MAINE STAY BED & BREAKFAST lettering blurred into the truck's Victorian colors.

The driver, Mr. Smith, turned around to look

through his rear window and see who his daughter was calling.

At that moment, Herbert Howe, who everyone in Camden knew was too senile to be driving, chose to putt out of Trim Street, onto Washington.

But he forgot to look both ways. Or even one way.

Behind the wheel, the old codger was like a horse wearing blinders.

By the time Mr. Smith's attention was back on the road, he was staring at the blue door of Herbert's 1960 Chevy Bel Air.

Way too close. About six feet away.

Adrenalin coursed through Smith's system.

His heart began to thud.

With extra oxygen to his brain, his senses sharpened and time seemed to slow.

Should he brake and chance skidding with the brakes locked?

He chose to steer right. Try to get around.

But, instead, the Model-A slid on slippery fall leaves.

Smith hit the brakes.

Lost control.

He overcorrected by jerking the steering wheel hard left.

Louise stared through the windshield, stiffened, and screamed, "Daddy, we're going to hit that pole!"

At the moment the Smith vehicle slammed into the utility pole, Herbert was a block away, oblivious.

He cut off a green Plymouth as he pulled out onto

Knowlton Street. On his good days, Herbert was about two sandwiches short of a picnic.

* * *

Blammmmm!

The Model-A's front end caved in as it impacted with the wooden pole. The car wheezed like a teakettle.

The pole cracked, quivered, teetered.

You could cut the silence with a knife.

Fascinated, horrified, Davey and Matt saw it all.

Davey went weak, boneless.

Matt reached down and rubbed at his bum leg, the one he'd broken the year before.

Mrs. Cross's front door flew open. She held the throat of her flannel robe tight as she curled around the storm door. "Godfrey almighty! What was that noise?"

Davey got his chin in gear. "Mrs. Cross, call nine-one-one. The Smiths' truck hit an electric pole."

"Tell 'em," Matt added, "a Ten-55 on Washington Street, corner of Trim."

While the EMS system was being activated, Matt and Davey — citizen responders — surveyed the scene.

Question number one: Was the scene safe?

They didn't know.

The two boys stood together, checking out the accident area.

They looked up. There was a tangle of wires at the cross arms of the pole.

Davey grabbed Matt's bicep, pointed. A wire was swinging directly above the Model-A. "We could have some major league electrical danger here, Portable-M," using Matt's Puckerbrush Rescue name.

"Ten-04, Portable-D," Matt concurred. "But the ground doesn't seem to be energized." They both concentrated on their feet. Nope, their soles weren't tingling. If they were, backing off — now! — would have been the move.

"Math-YEW?"

A voice from the truck.

"Matthew, are you here?" A slow-moving pink-clad shoulder stuck up. Then a mop of black curls.

Louise's face lifted.

Her usually quick eyes were flat as she focused out the side window. She was ghost-white.

Then she saw Matthew, back on the grass. "I'm . . ." she squirmed out of her shoulder harness and fumbled for the door handle, "getting out."

"NO, STAY PUT!" Matt ordered. "DON'T OPEN THAT DOOR LOUISE!"

The utility pole tottered, then fell forward, hanging up in the branches of a maple.

At the sound of falling timber, Louise hunched, wrapping her arms around her head.

One high-voltage wire, slung above the truck's cab, spewed sparks as it drooped in slow motion into the truck's bed.

Steam erupted from under the hood of the car.

30

"We've got to . . ." Mr. Smith's voice rose. "We've got to get out. The truck's on fire. Hurry!"

That's not fire, it's steam, thought Davey. *Maybe a cracked radiator. It's electricity they've got to worry about.*

"Portable-D," Matt spoke to Davey. "Go around — stay real wide — and deal with Mr. Smith. He's okay but he's *got* to stay put. I'll gentle Louise until EMS responds. Ten-03?"

"Ten-04, Portable-M," said Davey as he wove an arc, far from the truck with its high-voltage payload. He began to call to Louise's father as he jogged over: "Mr. Smith, don't move. There's a live wire touching your truck. The truck's hot, charged with electricity."

"What? Where?" This news made Mr. Smith *more* nervous, not less. "Louise, did you hear? Get out, little girl. Looks like the truck's on fire; the fuel tank might explode."

He glanced at the ominous steam again.

"Jump, Louise. Jump out, honey!"

*   *   *

Matt moved up to a position where Louise could see him, away from the truck. "Believe me, Louise, you're a lot safer inside the truck than trying to get out.

"I know your Dad's worried about fire," Matt's words were slow and easy, "but I don't think that's gonna happen. What he thinks is smoke, is really steam from a cracked radiator. No sweat.

"What you *do* need to worry about is the electric

31

line across the bed of the truck. It's in contact with the truck — the truck's hot, electrified, and so is everything in it.

"Right now," Matt's usually loud voice stayed low-key, "the electricity's bottled up. The rubber tires keep it from running into the ground. Which is great. But you can't let yourself be a bridge between the electricity and the ground."

'Cause it'll fry you as it travels through you, he thought but didn't say.

"But, Matthew, I'm touching the truck now." Louise recoiled as though singed by a burning candle. "What do I do?"

"Sit tight. You can touch the truck all you want. I know this sounds crazy, but the electricity won't hurt you as long as you stay in the truck. You just can't touch the ground at the same time you're touching the vehicle."

He hesitated. "Are you hurt at all?"

"Nope, I had a seat belt on. I'm okay."

"Good." Matt rubbed his knee. "Let's keep it that way. How's your dad doing? He calm down any?"

* * *

Davey's hawk eyes drilled into Mr. Smith's. "Stay put, sir."

But Mr. Smith wasn't seeing or hearing him. He was flashing back to Vietnam, back to the sixties.

His eyes were distant, glazed.

Davey watched as Mr. Smith threw open his door. Killing volts of electricity were lying in wait. As soon

32

as — *if* — he touched both the car and the ground at the same time, the electricity would be free . . . free to course through his body on its way to the ground.

Forget about burns.

As soon as one foot touched the ground, the current could leave the car, race along Mr. Smith's fingers and arms, zap his heart muscles as it streaked through his chest, down his legs, and into the street.

Davey had to stop this adult from inadvertently killing himself. How?

"Dad, don't do it. Stay in the car." Louise's voice held authority.

Mr. Smith paused, looked over his shoulder, and recognized his daughter. But the panic was still there, gnawing in his belly.

"Dad, I trust Matthew. If he says we're safer staying in the truck, then that's where we ought to stay."

"Louise, hon, maybe they're right. Maybe you're right. Are you okay? But I can't stay here. It's too . . . I'm gonna go crazy if I don't get out and get out now."

Turning to Davey, "Fire or no fire, I can't stay. I'm outta here."

The door was still open. He began to move.

* * *

"Wait, Mr. Smith. We've got to be real careful. It's okay to touch the ground. And it's okay to touch the truck. But not both at the same time. Got it?"

"Sure, that's not hard. I'll just step out." Mr. Smith

33

swung a leg over the doorsill and toward the ground.

"Stop!" Davey's voice was urgent. It was time to talk turkey. "That's exactly what you can't do — have a foot in the car, and a foot on the ground. If you're gonna do it safely, it's got to be my way."

The leg froze.

"It's okay, son. I've got my rubber duck-boots on. I'm insulated, so it's not like I'll be touching the ground."

His leg stuck out again.

"Geezum, Dad," Louise spoke up, "listen to Davey, will ya?"

Mr. Smith's foot stopped, this time an inch or so above the grass.

"If you gotta get out," she said, "fine. But pay attention. If you can't follow simple directions, how'd you get to be elected selectman?"

Mr. Smith turned his body to stare at his daughter. His stray left foot moved back up to the rocker panel.

Davey saw his chance.

"All right, Mr. Smith. Keep both feet on that rocker panel. Yeah, just like that. You're right that rubber insulates. But this current's too much.

"Now, grab ahold of the windshield on the right and the window post on the left.

"Next," Davey continued, "straighten up as best you can and, when I count to three, jump off with your feet high and push with your hands. *At the same time.*"

Mr. Smith nodded.

"Good. And try to land on both feet as far from the car as you can.

"Ready?"

"One." Davey paused.

"Two." He kept his eye on Mr. Smith's feet.

Mr. Smith rose off the seat into a crouch, like he was going to do a standing broad jump.

"Three."

Matthew's mouth drooped. He covered it with his hand. And watched.

Louise's fingertips pressed her lips as her father launched into the air, out and away from the truck.

Both feet landed, thump.

Mr. Smith lurched forward, reaching out for Davey's hand.

Davey, five feet away from the truck, took another step back. No way would he touch Louise's dad before every piece of his tumbling body and clothing was well clear of the truck.

Without support, Mr. Smith staggered into Davey's arms. The two of them collapsed in a heap.

Davey, trying to squirm out from under Mr. Smith, noticed a crisp, dark blue pant leg next to his face.

A strong voice from above said, "Okay, who can tell me what happened?" A first responder in the form of Police Officer Robby Laite was Ten-10. At the scene.

* * *

I'm late for school, Matt was thinking as Central Maine Power's line crew arrived, yellow lights flashing, on the heels of PD.

Standing in the middle of the street, Robby Laite waved arms, directed traffic around the Ten-55.

From their cherry picker, the utility emergency responders de-energized the wire.

Then they opened Louise's car door.

As she was helped out, she bent and twisted this way and that to make sure all her working parts were.

One of the CMP men took off his hard hat and spoke to Louise. "You did the right thing, young lady. It's a pleasure to meet such a clearheaded gal."

Davey watched as Louise's cheeks colored.

Louise's eyes were on Matt.

Matt, inspecting the wrecked Model-A, chose not to notice.

* * *

The police report was completed. Mr. Smith was waiting for John French's wrecker to arrive and Davey, Matt, and Louise were headed for school, just around the corner.

"We'll be about, . . ." predicted Matt as he looked at Davey's watch, "about an hour late."

"But what a *hot* excuse we have," said Davey.

As they turned into Knowlton Street, the blue Chevy Bel Air driven by Mr. Howe moved down the center line at about three miles an hour. Herbert Howe smiled over his steering wheel.

Matt watched the old man's retreating car. "That old coot," he said, throwing his hands up in the air.

"Matthew?" Louise started, then halted. Cleared her throat. "Matthew, I want to thank you for being so . . . so . . . *there*." She looked at him with bird-bright eyes. "My father could be dead now. Probably would be. You're a real hero."

"No big deal, Louise. Say Davey," Matt turned back to his cousin, "I never finished telling you about *Avalanche*. That's a book I just read, Louise, you probably wouldn't like it. . . . So anyway, Davey, here's this coyote, and the kid in the book — Chris — decides to shoot it *BOOM!* when all of a sudden an awesome wall of snow . . ."

For such a slick kid, mused Davey, *my cousin's as dumb as a cobblestone when it comes to Louise.*

SKILL
Hot Wires and Vehicle Safety

WHAT is it? Knowing what to do for yourself and others when a car, truck, or bus is in contact with an electrical wire.

WHY do you do it? To avoid electrocution. Electricity wants to move from place to place, from wires to ground. So, once a downed wire energizes a car, the vehicle's metal holds the electricity looking for a way out. It can't leave through the rubber tires. They are thick insulators, blocking the electrical flow. It *can* exit through, and injure, a person.

WHEN do you do it? When a vehicle and electrical wire might be touching each other.

HOW do you do it? Make it clear that, even though the car is charged with electricity, it is safest to remain inside. If the vehicle is on fire or someone refuses to stay put, as Louise's father did, then you need to consider talking them out of the car. *This is a last resort.* Keep far away from the energized vehicle and wires, as you: 1) Calm the person and explain the situation. 2) Instruct them to open the door. 3) Tell them to turn their body sideways on the seat. 4) They should then brace themselves in the door opening. 5) Now it is time for them to push off, leap-

ing far clear of the vehicle. 6) Land on *both* feet.
7) You keep far back.

Is the scene safe?

Keep away from downed wires, even if someone other than a professional rescuer tells you they're harmless.

Never touch, kick, or move a downed wire. With anything.

Wires do not have to be sparking to be deadly.

Don't ever touch a car that might be energized.

Never offer a hand to someone inside of or leaping from an energized car.

* * *

To learn more about energized wires, read *The Story of Electricity* by Mae and Ira Freeman, published by Random House, 1961.

Emergency Rescue! Report

Report number 7	My name *Davey Mountain*

Incident location
Trim and Washington
street
Camden , Maine
city/town   state

My address
Sea Street
street
Camden , ME 04843
city/town   state   zip

Was the scene safe? yes ☐ no ☒
Describe the scene. *On electrical wire was in contact with the truck The truck was HOT !!!!*

First name of victim *Mr. Smith and Louise* **Age** *36 and 14* male ☒ female ☒

Aid first given by
☒ me *and Matt*
☐ someone else
☐ EMTs
☐ police
☐ firefighters

Transported to *(no one was hurt)*

Describe any transportation or communication problems. *none*

Type of illness or injury or accident
☐ bone fracture
☐ aches and sprains
☐ bleeding injury
☐ illness
☐ fire
☐ auto or truck accident
☐ water incident
☐ HazMat
☐ airplane disaster
☐ lost person/search and rescue
☐ extrication
☐ animal incident
☒ electrical accident
☐ tornado
☐ hurricane
☐ blizzard
☐ other

Who called for help?
☐ me
☐ a friend
☐ family member
☐ professional responder
☒ neighbor
☐ other person

Emergency responders on the scene
☐ EMTs
☐ firefighters
☒ police
☐ HazMat
☐ emergency department
☒ utility crew
☐ search and rescue

Describe what happened, and the outcome. Include unusual circumstances. *I talked Mr. Smith out of the truck, and Matt talked down Louise , so they both weren't electrocuted*

my signature *Davey Mountain*

3
Crack

"It says here in the *Courier*," Matt Rich poked at the headline for emphasis, "that a fourteen-year-old girl from Bethel was trapped in the cab when her father's truck fell through pond ice, and was underneath for forty minutes. . . . Whoa. . . . 'So far this winter six people have died when their vehicles sank.' "

Davey Mountain, perched above the sports section spread over the Oriental rug, didn't answer. He was reading about the latest Windjammer basketball loss.

Bossy, Davey's bulldog, headed for the downstairs bathroom. Neither Davey nor Matt heard him slopping a drink of water from the toilet.

"Matt, listen to this." Davey read aloud. " 'The United States Toboggan Championships will be held this weekend at Camden's Snow Bowl.' Wouldn't it be neat if we tuned your dad's old toboggan and won that huge trophy?" He read another couple of paragraphs. " 'Camden's Chamber of Commerce director stated that the pond ice is soft today. It must be hardened for the chute to be utilized, as the toboggans slide out onto the pond to brake. But they're sure,' " Davey continued, " 'it will freeze solid overnight and be safe by morning. Everyone's home tuning . . .' "

"Hmmm." Matt examined a shot of the Bethel accident and the victim's school photo. "They say she's critical." He looked at his cousin. "You know all those guys that race their trucks on the ice in Warren? I guess that's wicked dangerous."

"Maa-att." Davey shook his section of the paper at his cousin. "Check it out. We could win the championship! Probably would have to practice some, though. Hey, Susan could help us tune."

Susan Baer, Davey's friend and neighbor, was a competition downhill skier, and was savvy about making skis m-o-v-e.

Matt's head was over the front page. "They say, if this Bethel girl survives, she might not have any brain damage because of the cold water shutting down her body."

Davey glanced at the outside thermometer: 18°F. The unseasonable January weather seemed past. "I bet that ice's just hard enough to practice. . . ."

The cousins leaned against the feather-filled sofa that faced a wall of windows at the back of Davey's house. The sun-filled space looked out on Camden harbor.

The fleet of windjammer sailing ships, which in summertime took guests on week-long cruises in and out of the craggy Penobscot Bay islands, lay at its moorings. Masts were bare of sails. Decks and cabins were wrapped in plastic, like greenhouses, so on all but the coldest of days the crew could work on the interiors.

To the south, Captain Moore rowed around *Surprise* checking ice boards he'd nailed to his schooner's waterline. Once the harbor ice arrived, the wood would protect the big ship's sleek green hull as she bobbed up and down.

"Can't you see the toboggan trophy sitting over there?" Davey nodded toward the granite mantel above the walk-in fireplace towering against the room's east wall. "Or, better still, I bet it'd fit on my bookshelf. I could keep it for a month then you could keep it."

"Trophy?" Matt looked toward the mantel. "What trophy?"

"Boys." Davey's father came down the stairs from his office above. "I'm headed out to the Snow Bowl with Chief Oxton on Engine Six. We're going to hose down the toboggan chute. Wanna come?"

The boys made eye contact. Davey winked.

"No, thanks, Dad," Davey told him. "We've got some work to do over at Matt's."

* * *

43

At the same time Mr. Mountain wrestled with a 1½-inch hose, spraying a fog-like pattern of water over the toboggan chute, Matt, Susan, and Davey were buzzing like bees over the six-foot-long toboggan in the back of Matt's barn.

Matt's big square fingers worked sandpaper along the slats as Susan warmed her special downhill ski-racing wax. Davey was choosing a paintbrush for wax application.

The sled hadn't seen the light of day for years, not since Matt's dad had bought the diner. Matt could remember his sister, Stacy, and himself sledding down the hills out in Appleton. But that was way before Stacy left for the University of Maine.

At least five years ago, maybe more.

A couple of screws were missing. The pull rope had to be replaced. And everything needed scrubbing and sanding. No big deal.

"Matt." Davey glanced over the list of rules he'd ripped out of the *Courier*. "Says some kind of a cushion is required. What about using the old sleeping bag over there?"

The wax was ready. All three stood over the toboggan as Susan began stroking it on.

As Matt's father, Mr. Rich, walked through on his way to work, Matt was taping a stopwatch to the front curl of the toboggan.

"Matt, I hope you're not thinking about going tobogganing at the Snow Bowl tonight. The pond ice is uncertain after the warm weather. And you boys

44

don't know how to read it." Mr. Rich looked over his glasses. "I don't want any of you out there until Jack Williams up to the Snow Bowl announces it's safe, hear?"

* * *

The toboggan was a living thing, a ribbon of life. *Had it lost contact with the ice-coated wooden chute,* Matt wondered? *Could it fly?*

The pull of gravity sucked the sled downhill.

Its individual slats rippled up and down as they skidded over bits of snow granules.

There was no sound. Or a world of noise. Matt wasn't sure which.

"Eeeeeeeeeeeeyowwww!"

From the back of the sled behind Susan, Davey's scream was bloodcurdling, like he'd just turned to find Freddie Kreuger sitting behind him.

Matt hoped Davey hadn't fallen off, but he was too busy hanging on for dear life himself to stew over it. Or to turn and look.

* * *

Before this first run when, under the cover of darkness, the three had pussyfooted into the toboggan chute area of the Snow Bowl, Matt hadn't known what to expect. He did know that the sled was as tuned as they could get it without a trial run.

He had remembered Louise cornering him one day after last year's races and telling him how her toboggan's bottom had been worn smooth in places, with the wax rubbed off the high spots.

45

Matt, Davey, and Susan wanted their toboggan to be as perfect as possible, with no sticky high spots. It was Matt who suggested they sneak out tonight and run it just once. Quick and dirty. Check it out. They'd be home before anyone knew they were gone.

That run was dynamite in terms of fun, but their time was slow, 9.97 seconds.

They had decided to try again, after Susan did a little magical tuning.

One more run wouldn't hurt anything.

Matt beat his crossed arms against his shoulders to keep warm in the 18° temperature while Susan fussed. He wished the warming shed wasn't locked so they could get out of the wind for a minute. His breath came out in puffs of frozen ice crystals.

A full moon was rising over the top of Bald Mountain. Its light shimmered on the icy surface of Hosmer Pond. The summer cottages were dark. The nearest visible sign of life was the outside light of the Spencer place, a half-mile up the Barnstown Road.

Matt and Davey donned their Puckerbrush Rescue headlamps for some light up the slippery slope to the starting gate.

With Davey and Susan on one side and Matt on the other, the three held on to the side rope of the six-foot-long toboggan. Matt had draped the sleeping bag cushion over his shoulders.

At the top of the frozen trail, five wooden stairs led up to the deck surrounding the gate. As Matt stepped onto the first stair, the wood creaked the way it does when it's really cold. The ice had to be safe. For sure.

At the top, they laid the toboggan into the launch platform. As Matt bent and smoothed the sleeping bag between the side ropes, he glanced down. The pond seemed a long way away . . . and an awful lot lower. "Who's first on?" he asked, standing up. "Davey?"

Davey shook his head. "You ought to be, Big Matt, to give it front weight. Then Susan, and then me."

Matt looked at him. "Hey, you go first. It was *your* idea."

"Are you two birds," Susan's bubbly voice floated out, "at it again? Hey, I'll be first, or last. I don't care." She glanced down, raring to go. "This is a piece of cake. I stand at the top of a double diamond at Sugarloaf and I can't even *see* where it ends. NBD. All we've got to do is hang on."

Susan plopped down on the toboggan. Somebody had to get things started.

Matt sat down in front of Susan and tucked his feet up under the stopwatch. He doubled over as far as he could between his knees and grabbed the ropes on either side.

Behind him, Susan leaned forward, tucking her legs around his waist.

Matt let go of the rope and rubbed his knee. Funny that his old injury would start to hurt now.

Must be the cold weather.

Davey scrunched onto what was left of the sled. He swung his legs so they rested on top of Susan's and his boots ended up in Matt's lap.

Davey reached behind him. His butt was hanging over the end. Tight fit. He scrunched it in.

Just before reaching for the ropes, Davey one-eighty'd the visor of his Red Sox cap so it wouldn't get caught by the wind.

"Davey." Matt was calling the shots. "You release the gate. Okay, on the count of three."

Matt let go of the rope with his left hand and got set to click the start of the stopwatch.

"One!"

Matt tucked his head down between his knees.

"Two!"

Susan leaned over Matt's stretched back. She turned her head sideways and rested it against the PUCKERBRUSH RESCUE SQUAD jacket lettering.

Davey's fingers tightened around the lever that would release the seesaw-like launch platform, tipping the nose of their toboggan into the chute.

"Three!"

Davey pulled back on the start lever.

One second the toboggan was level. The next, it was pointed downhill at a forty-five-degree angle.

Matt's stomach was still up above.

His hand blindly clicked the stopwatch.

The toboggan shot like a bullet down the barrel of a pistol.

It picked up speed. A lot of speed.

Matt knew that with every bit of wind resistance he could eliminate, the faster they'd go. More speed? Did he really want to lay it on?

He tucked in his elbows, lowered his head.

The muscles in his curved back stretched tight. They weren't designed to hold this position for long.

Thwap. Matt's elbow whomped the chute's side. The sled was off the fall line — the straightest, fastest route downhill.

Thwump. Before he could adjust, they ricocheted off the other side.

Matt shifted his weight.

Susan pressed tighter into the curl of his back. Her knees pulled in to his ribs.

Out of the corner of his eye, Matt saw tree trunks whizzing by.

They were picking up speed. Still.

It was fantastic.

Whoosh! At the bottom of the run, the metal timing wands flashed past as Matt clicked the stopwatch.

Then there was a dip in the chute with a leap off the end out onto the frozen ice of Hosmer Pond.

Matt's eyes lifted to the stopwatch: 9.37 seconds. Wicked fast.

All that was left was the run-out. The sled cork-screwed as it lost speed on the slick pond ice.

* * *

Matt dragged the heels of his Merrells on the smooth ice.

As the friction slowed the toboggan, Matt remembered his dad's warning. *Once again,* he thought, *Dad's wrong. He's such a worrywart.*

Matt couldn't wait to tell him how strong the ice was.

His smile soured when he realized that, if his father ever found out, he'd come down hard on him.

The ice groaned, as if in agreement.

Matt shook his father out of his head, and hopped up next to Susan who was straightening Davey's crooked headlamp off his ears and back up on his forehead.

Davey flipped on the switch.

Something didn't feel right under their soles. They looked down; the light shone on their feet and the edge of the toboggan.

In the circle of glow, they saw it. The ice was dished — sagging with their weight, as if three rocks were piled in the center of a trampoline.

The ice was the trampoline. They were the rocks.

All around them, the no-longer-smooth ice was rippling in expanding circles, like water moves when its surface is disturbed.

Susan and Matt stared as Davey moved his light further afield.

Then they recognized it. The sound of cracking ice.

"Quick. Move apart," Davey ordered, his hawk eyes surveying the scene. "Spread our weight."

As they sprinted for firm ground, Davey's headlamp picked up spidered ice areas all over the place.

Rumbling sounds followed their movement.

More ripples.

The ice was flowing. Moving. Pushed down by their weight, it sprang back when they moved on.

Matt tried to float over the ice. It felt like he was running on water.

He was.

Ten feet from shore, Davey's foot broke through. A circle of black water, released from the ice's pressure, gushed out of the jagged hole.

Matt, towing the toboggan, yelled, "Don't stop Davey, you're almost there."

Davey yanked his boot out, kept going.

Susan leapt off the ice. "Terra firma," she sighed. The hard ground felt nice and firm.

Three, maybe four more strides — Davey'd have it.

Matt watched from land as his cousin's next step sank below the surface. Davey tottered. Swayed.

Davey tried to regain balance, tried to stay up on the ice.

Matt bit his lip.

Davey began to topple.

"Daaaavey!!" Matt's voice filled the night air as his cousin disappeared, face first.

Through the dark water and ice, Matt saw Davey's headlamp die.

* * *

"What? Where is he? What's happened?" Susan, off to the side, had missed the action.

Before Matt could answer, Davey's head popped up. Then his shoulders and chest.

51

He was sitting in about a foot of water.

Within minutes, his body was defending itself from the cold 38° water. Gradually all of Davey was tightening, hugging onto any remaining body heat. A gasp squeezed out of him.

As his chest and belly muscles began to constrict, his lungs felt smaller. He panted.

The shell of his body tried to warm itself up by shaking-exercising. Davey began to shiver.

Matt flicked on his headlamp. He walked toward the ghostlike face of his cousin. "Hey, Davey. You still okay? We were almost in deep sneakers."

Davey just sat, glazed.

"Come on, Davey." Matt held onto Susan as he offered Davey his hand. "Let's get you outta there."

"Davey. Stand up," Susan coaxed. "You need to get warm."

"Wait. Where's my cap?" He sounded drunk. "I need my cap." He fished around in the water.

Matt scratched his wool hat. *Davey's sitting in ice water, he's freezing and worried about his Red Sox cap?*

"For goodness' sakes, forget your — " Before Susan could finish, Matt had grabbed Davey, and pulled him up and out.

Davey, limp as a dishrag, didn't help.

Davey fumbled with his fly. His fingers didn't work.

"I gotta go." Davey sounded pained. "Oops. I just did."

Susan looked at him. He didn't seem to care.

Matt stared at Davey. Why was he acting like such a wing nut?

Omagosh.

Mentally, Matt slapped his forehead — he'd almost missed the signs and symptoms.

Hypothermia. A classic case. Davey's body was losing the battle to keep warm.

The cold was slowing everything up. Even his thinking. Davey was irrational because his brain wasn't getting enough oxygen pumped up by his sluggish, chilled heart.

Matt put it all together.

The gasp.

Davey's panting — hyperventilating. Which made him short on oxygen.

Pale face.

Slurred speech.

Shivering. Body trying to move to make heat.

Feet and hands not working right?

Not surprising since his system was intent on protecting his vital core: brain, spinal cord, heart, lungs — all his precious bodily parts. So his legs and arms were left with cooler blood. Feet? Forget it. Hands? Their heat moved into the body core.

And now his having to go. Davey was vasoconstricting — the blood vessels in his skin were closing; veins and arteries squeezed dry like a sponge. Blood, water — *everything* was pushed into his body's center. No wonder his kidneys and bladder were loaded with fluid.

"Mild hypothermia." Matt knew if Davey's condition continued to get worse — if he wasn't warmed — cold challenge would win. His body furnace would be overwhelmed and hypothermia would set in.

Hypothermia kills.

Is the scene safe? Matt asked himself.

No way, he decided. *I'm wet from hauling Davey in. Susan must be freezing, too. We both gotta get warm. Davey too. Stat.*

"I wanna-get-bac-inna-water," Davey whined. "S'warrmer. . . ." He started to unzip his jacket. "Wind's cold."

"Can't let you do that," said Matt. He knew that the pond's water, which would feel warmer to Davey, would draw heat out of him twenty-five times faster than air.

Davey started to crawl to the pond, then seemed to forget where he was headed.

Matt's sweat was running, although he was shrammed through with cold. "Susan, we've got a dire medical emergency here. Davey's reacting to intense cooling. The next stage, severe hypothermia, is a killer. Run for help. I'll try to warm him."

Susan was off.

* * *

Matt spread out the sleeping bag. Then he removed Davey's clothes, and got him to lie in the middle.

Davey, now naked, was still moaning about Matt wanting to undress him — "No, Matt. Don't take off my jacket" — as Matt zipped his cousin up in the mummy bag.

"It's okay, Davey. Your clothes aren't doing you any good." Once wet, they'd lost about all their insulating ability. But he didn't waste time trying to explain.

Matt pulled the face-hole's drawstring tight. "There," he gentled his cousin. "Now you won't lose ninety percent of your heat through your noggin. Not much fat up there to insulate you, bonehead."

Matt looked at Davey to see if he got a response. Hard to tell. All that could be seen of Davey was a nose.

What else can I do? Matt asked himself.

Let's see. . . . First, cold reduction. I took off his wet duds, then blocked the air's cold challenge with the sleeping bag.

Maybe I should place him on the toboggan, to keep him off the frozen ground?

He did it.

Another way to reduce the cold challenge is to warm the air around him. Build a fire? Tough, but do-able. I'll do everything else I can, and if EMTs aren't yet Ten-10, I'll work on a fire till they arrive.

Second. Heat retention. I'm keeping in the heat he's got by sticking him in the sleeping bag. The bag is pull-stringed so it covers his head and most of his face.

Heat production is third. Davey needs fuel for a different kind of fire. He needs food to produce heat, so he'll warm from the inside out. He needs to eat stuff easy for his body to burn fast. Simple sugars. Like hot chocolate, sweet junk food. Candy bar.

I have to watch him as he eats, Matt reminded himself. *Davey was acting weird and could choke due to his altered mental state.*

Matt searched through Davey's pockets.

A Toblerone. Davey's favorite food, Swiss chocolate.

He popped a small piece into Davey's mouth. Davey chewed and swallowed it okay. Good. Matt fueled up, too, took a bite.

Davey opened his mouth for another piece, like a baby bird.

Matt sat and watched Davey munch. He still looked blue, but his shivering had slowed. Great.

Wait a minute. Which is it? wondered Matt. *If he's getting warmer, he'd stop that automatic exercise his body's been doing. It'd be no longer necessary.*

But if he's going down the tubes into severe hypothermia, he'll also stop shivering. Because his body's shutting down. Dying. . . .

He looked through the darkness for Susan. Anyone.

He turned back to Davey.

Time to use his own personal furnace to heat Davey, and to get out of the cold himself.

Matt got into the sleeping bag.

As Matt lay there hugging him, he felt Davey begin to shiver again.

Matt started to cry.

* * *

Susan had a different, and effective, way of getting warm. She'd run as fast as her skier-legs could carry her down the Barnstown Road until she'd spotted her neighbor's car, then flagged it down.

Now she sat in the station wagon, watching Mrs. Murphy punch in *-7-7 on her car phone.

Within seven minutes, Puckerbrush Rescue Squad was Ten-10 at the edge of Hosmer Pond. EMTs placed heat packs on Davey's groin, underarms, and neck. A space blanket that looked like a huge piece of aluminum foil encapsulated him, reflecting his own body-heat.

Ten minutes after that, Davey was rewrapped in cozy flannel blankets from the warming cabinet at Penobscot Bay Hospital's emergency department.

Twelve minutes later, Mrs. Murphy, Susan and Matt, and Davey's, Matt's, and Susan's parents were at the hospital, too.

Mr. Rich, Matt's dad, looked worried. Then, when he heard that Davey was fine, he got angry.

They were all in their respective homes by midnight.

Davey dreamt that he was a frostbitten Arctic explorer.

After a restless night for both of them, Davey and Matt were lazing around in Davey's living room.

Davey, lying on the sofa, sipped sweet cocoa. The sun shining through the windows made a square design on the thick Hudson's Bay blanket covering him.

He still wasn't warm.

". . . *The top ten toboggans are lined up . . .*" — the radio was on — "*. . . for the final run in the one-man . . .*"

Hours before, Davey's and Matt's parents and Matt's sister, Stacy, had piled into Stacy's VW bus and headed for the races.

Davey had to stay home, keep warm, and drink hot liquids. Doctor's orders.

Matt had some orders, too — from his father. He was to stay by Davey and make sure the patient did what he was supposed to.

The boys were probably the only people still in town.

". . . *now the time to beat in the two-man race is nine point twenty-seven. . . .*" REAL COUNTRY 103.3 FM was on hand with a sled-by-sled account. Matt wondered why, since everyone except him and Davey were out there.

They listened, and read the newspaper.

"Look at this, Davey." Matt shoved his section under Davey's nose.

Girl Dies After
Pond Accident

Although she had been expected to survive, Linda Robbins, 14, of Bethel, who suffered from severe hypothermia after being trapped under ice for forty minutes, died yesterday. According to a Bethel Hospital spokeswoman, the Bethel Middle School student took a turn for the worse yesterday morning. She never awoke from her coma.

"*. . . All right, folks,*" the radio announcer's voice rose, "*we're ready for the three-man toboggan race. The ten finalists are lined up at the top of the run. The Camden Tannery's team will be first down the chute, followed by Puckerbrush Rescue, then . . .*"

Matt rubbed the corner of his mouth with his thumb.

"*. . . The time to beat is nine point forty seconds. The final entry, the Smith family, is approaching the starting gate. . . .*"

Matt closed his eyes. Their time last night bettered the 9.40. They'd be winning, in line for the trophy, if they were racing. He could kick himself for not listening to his dad. Everything was all Matt's fault.

". . . Unbelievable, the Smiths win by two-hundredths of a second. Nine point thirty-eight! Their daughter Louise is jumping up and down. . . ."

"Oh jeez," Davey groaned.

"Louise?" Matt couldn't stand it.

SKILL
Reading Pond and Lake Ice

WHAT is it? Understanding how safe ice is before you step on it.

WHY do you do it? For your own safety. Rescuing someone who has fallen through ice is extremely difficult, and often unsuccessful. Even if a person is rescued, the effects of frigid water can kill.

WHEN do you do it? Whenever you encounter new, untested ice. Never assume that, because the weather is cold, the ice is safe. That's what got Davey, Matt, and Susan into trouble.

HOW do you do it? Check the thickness of clear, blue ice on lakes and ponds, and use this Ice Strength Guide to understand what weights ice can support.

Ice Thickness	Permissable Load
2"	One person on foot
3"	Group, in single file
7½"	Passenger car
8"	Light truck
10"	Medium truck
12"	Heavy truck

River ice, with water running underneath, is weaker than lake or pond ice. *Never* go on slush ice, snow ice, buckled ice or pressure ridges, or saltwater ice. Ice over currents, shallows, and springs will be thinner — and dangerous.

Is the scene safe?

Test ice before walking on it.

If you can't measure it yourself, check with local authorities.

If you can't measure it and no one else knows for sure, keep off.

If you don't KNOW, don't GO.

* * *

To learn more about ice safety, read *Sailing on Ice* by Jack Andresen, published by A.S. Barnes and Co., Inc., 1974.

Emergency Rescue! Report

Report number **8**	My name MATT RICH

Incident location OFF BARNSTOWN ROAD street (HOSMER POND) CAMDEN, MAINE city/town state	My address BAY VIEW STREET street CAMDEN, ME 04843 city/town state zip

Was the scene safe?   yes   no (BUT WE THOUGHT SO.)
Describe the scene.   ☐   ☒

THE ICE WAS TOO THIN TO BE ON. IT WAS PROBABLY

ABOUT 2 INCHES THICK

First name of victim DAVEY	Age 14	male ☒	female ☐	Aid first given by ☒ me ☐ someone else ☐ EMTs ☐ police ☐ firefighters

Transported to
PENOBSCOT BAY HOSPITAL

Describe any transportation SUSAN WAS LUCKY
or communication problems. TO FIND SOMEONE
WITH A CAR PHONE.

Type of illness or injury or accident

- ☐ bone fracture
- ☐ aches and sprains
- ☐ bleeding injury
- ☒ illness   Hypothermia
- ☐ fire
- ☐ auto or truck accident
- ☐ water incident
- ☐ HazMat
- ☐ airplane disaster
- ☐ lost person/search and rescue
- ☐ extrication
- ☐ animal incident
- ☐ electrical accident
- ☐ tornado
- ☐ hurricane
- ☐ blizzard
- ☐ other

Who called for help?

- ☐ me
- ☒ a friend SUSAN
- ☐ family member
- ☐ professional responder
- ☒ neighbor Mrs. MURPHY
- ☐ other person

Emergency responders on the scene

- ☒ EMTs
- ☐ firefighters
- ☐ police
- ☐ HazMat
- ☐ emergency department
- ☐ utility crew
- ☐ search and rescue

Describe what happened, and the outcome. Include unusual
circumstances. DAVE FELL THROUGH THE ICE AND GOT
SOAKING WET. AIR TEMP. WAS 18° - COLD
CHALLENGE! THEN HE GOT MILD HYPOTHERMIA.
I HAD TO REWARM HIM.

my signature *Matt Rich*

4
Cut

Six-year-old Butch lost a large amount of blood in a short amount of time.

Davey saw the little kid blanch. The white sleeve of his turtleneck was drenched red. Blood, running off the tips of his fingers, was mixing with drizzling rain.

Hemorrhage.

Davey's head spun, searching for help, even though he knew he'd see only apple trees. What did he expect, smack in the middle of an orchard?

Why did he ever agree to baby-sit Butch, the orchard owners' nephew, in the first place?

But there wasn't time to think about himself. If he didn't do something, Butch would bleed to death.

* * *

It had all started at about 8:00 that morning when Mr. Anderson called from Hope Orchards. Davey had reached over his bowl of Müeslix and picked up the kitchen phone.

"Hello, Davey? How have you been? What's up? How're your folks?" Mr. Anderson spoke in question marks. "Any chance you'd do some work for us this afternoon?"

Davey considered his options. His Saturday chores were done — Bossy'd had his flea dip and the second-floor bathroom had been scrubbed. Homework? He could do that anytime.

The extra cash'd be nice. Davey was saving for a slick Black Diamond rock climbing harness they had over at Maine Sport.

And Davey enjoyed working side by side with the Andersons in their 6,500-tree apple orchard out in Hope. Last winter, while they pruned, he'd been the one who fed cut-off limbs into their chopper. This year he'd planted a new block with them, a couple of hundred Cortland apple trees.

He looked forward to picking — and eating — the green reddish-purple Cortlands four years from now, when the trees were mature enough to harvest.

"Sure, Mr. Anderson, I could do that."

"Remember my brother and sister-in-law?" Mr. Anderson questioned. "And their son, Butch? Don't you think it'd be nice if we showed 'em a good time this trip, take 'em out on *Betselma* and let them see lobster traps pulled?"

Davey knew those other Andersons, the ones from Boston. Last winter while they were helping in the orchard, Davey'd exchanged Red Sox info with them while little Butch ran around in circles.

"Know those Cortlands we planted? Think you could put guards on 'em? And watch Butch at the same time?"

Davey's hawk eyes narrowed. Tree guards and Butch, all at the same time. Davey found baby-sitting about as exciting as watching paint dry.

Mr. Anderson threw in a few more questions. When he stopped, Davey snuck in his own. "What do you need the tree guards for, Mr. Anderson?"

"Mice like to eat young trees' bark. The vermin gnaw as high as they can, leaving a barkless ring all the way around." Mr. Anderson tended to get out of his question-mode when he talked about his trees. "Once the tree's girdled that way, water and nutrients can't travel up. The supply's cut off. Tree dies. So we protect them with plastic sleeves, down on the ground."

The Andersons were neat people to work for. Apple growing was interesting. And besides, Davey liked most little kids.

"Sure, Mr. Anderson. Be happy to."

* * *

With Butch romping at his side, Davey set out from the Andersons' farmhouse.

First stop the apple barn.

Davey picked up the cardboard box filled with tree guards packed inside a plastic bag.

"What's that?" Butch hadn't taken a break from asking questions. Stacked in a corner of the barn were razor-sharp saws, cutters, and loppers. "Can I go see them?"

All winter, the Andersons worked the orchard thinning their trees so sunlight would get through, and air could circulate. They pruned to keep their trees short, too, so they could be harvested from the ground rather than from ladders. The Andersons didn't just let trees grow — they fertilized, sprayed, mowed year-round. They were advocates of modern management.

"Get away from those tools, Butch. No sense in your getting pruned." This was going to be a long afternoon.

Davey stopped to study a rough pencil map nailed inside the barn door. The orchard was so massive that he couldn't find where the New Cortlands were without checking the diagram. His eyes roamed. There were the Quinns in their block. . . . And the Summer block. . . . The entire orchard was divided into nicknamed neighborhoods of apple groups. Beyond-the-wall block. Pick-your-own block.

He found the New Cortland block way out in the back of the orchard.

The tree-guard box balanced on his shoulder, Davey headed out as Butch continued to ask questions.

As they moved toward the orchard, Davey answered about one out of four in his calm voice.

"How come the grass is so high? What's this yellow flower?"

They tramped through tall buttercups growing between lines of trees bursting with blossoms.

In a couple of weeks, those fruit flowers would be miniature apples.

After the June drop, when the tiniest apples fall to the ground, the remaining fruit would grow into robust red, yellow, and green spheres. Ready to be shipped worldwide.

Davey and Butch wove through row after row of forty varieties of trees. Davey still couldn't tell the difference between one tree and another. Golden Delicious looked like McIntosh looked like Baldwins.

"Can I have a drink of water?" Butch held his throat and let his tongue waggle.

Enjoying questions more than answers, he asked another. "What's that big hill over there?"

"That's Hatchet Mountain, Butch." Rain clouds clumped behind the mountain.

"Why're we walking this way? When's lunch? Where're the cows on this farm?"

As they walked around the splayed end of an apple-picking ladder, Butch was talking ten-to-a-dozen. "Why's this funny ladder's bottom fat?" He stopped, shielded his eyes with his hand, and squinted up at the wooden ladder's narrowing top rungs.

Davey explained how that smaller end fit between branches.

Then they turned into a row of healthy young trees, the Cortlands Davey'd helped plant. They sort of made Davey feel like a father. Or Johnny Appleseed?

Davey slung the box of guards to the ground and undid the twistie on the plastic bag.

"What do tree guards look like?" Butch wanted to know.

Davey pulled out a sheet of flexible white plastic the size of a license plate. It looked like someone had punched lines of holes in it.

He placed it around the first tree in the row and fastened the ends together to make a collar.

* * *

As Davey installed what must have been his hundredth tree guard, he hadn't a clue that the quiet of the orchard was about to be shattered.

All Davey knew was that his back hurt. He stood, pressing on it with his fingertips.

He thought he felt a drop of rain. Was it sprinkling?

Davey's keen green eyes surveyed the scene as he held out his palm. *Nothin'.* The drops, he decided, must be as far apart as chips in a store-bought cookie.

"Is it sprinkling, Davey?" Butch again, staring up at his idol.

A quick smile crossed Davey's face as he looked down at the boy. It'd reached the point where he and the kid were asking the same questions.

Davey winked at him. Butch winked back. With both eyes.

Mac ran over Davey's boot, followed by Tosh. The orchard's two chipmunks, named by the Andersons, always seemed to show up when Davey was out there.

Butch's face lit up. He was after them like a dragster, spinning his wheels on the damp grass.

Wonder how the four Andersons are doing on the lobster boat Betselma, mused Davey as he encircled a trunk at ground level with a guard. *Hope their parade doesn't get rained on.*

He looked to the east, toward the sea. The sky was blue over there.

Butch ran after Mac and Tosh, around a limb left over from pruning cleanup.

Mac hid under the downed branch. Tosh raced toward a neighboring block.

Butch stood, looking in one direction, then in the other.

Davey sighed, leaned over, and picked up a guard.

Butch, behind him, shrieked as Tosh came back toward Mac.

They rounded the tree where Davey knelt.

Davey bent the guard in his hand into a U-shape.

"Whyn't you wait?" Butch yelled to Mac and Tosh as they both ran into the Northern Spy block.

The guard in place, Davey glanced up. Butch, at top speed, had run to the end of the row, spun around, and was barreling back.

70

Actually, Davey thought, *this isn't bad. Earning double pay, while Mac and Tosh are doing all the baby-sitting work.*

Except answering Butch's endless questions.

"Hey guys, can't you slow down? Why don't you let me catch you? Don't you like me? How come you're so fast with such short legs?"

Davey reached into the box and pulled out the last guard. A raindrop hit the back of his neck.

Behind him, Butch's sneaks slipped out from under him.

His arms flew out to catch himself on the trunk ahead.

As Davey wrapped the guard around, a strange silence overtook him, as if it were a scream.

Butch's wrist hit the tree. A stub from a pruned branch jutting off the trunk pierced his skin.

Davey's spine tingled.

He kept working.

The branch stub sank like a spear into the soft, white inside of Butch's wrist.

Butch jerked back off the jagged end, sat up, grasped his arm.

The stillness continued. Davey, uncomfortable but not knowing why, stood and turned toward Butch.

Davey felt he'd been hit in the chest with a log. He saw the gaping hole below where Butch's thumb held his forearm.

Then it vanished as red oozed into it.

71

Within seconds, there was so much blood that it looked like a pig slaughter.

The silence ended as six-year-old Butch squealed.

Davey, trying to breathe, was shock-still.

* * *

Blood dripped off Butch's fingertips onto the ground. *Get a grip*, Davey warned himself, fighting back panic. *We've got*, he shuddered, *a situation here.*

Butch has cut either an artery or a vein.

If it's a vein, the blood would be dark red, almost purple.

Davey could see the blood was red. Really red. Like the color of the flag.

And if a vein had been pierced, blood would flow slow and steady.

Blood was pulsating out of Butch. Not flowing. Like it was being pumped.

Davey had to face facts. The stub had punched a hole through the artery in Butch's wrist.

This was an arterial bleed. Uncontrolled.

Butch was losing a large amount of blood in a short amount of time — hemorrhage!

The loop of Butch's circulatory system was broken. His oxygen-rich arterial blood was dumping onto the grass.

That oxygen wasn't going to get delivered.

But Butch's whole body *needed* that O_2.

And his vein and artery tubes needed the blood's bulk to fill them, to stay open, plumped up. If this blood-carrying system collapsed, Butch would be a goner.

Within three minutes.

The flow had to be staunched.

By Davey. Alone.

Davey whipped his PUCKERBRUSH RESCUE SQUAD T-shirt over his head, rolled it into a pad the size of a Big Mac . . . and stopped.

Is the scene safe? he asked himself just in time.

He grimaced. *No way, not with all this blood.*

Like all rescuers, Davey's first charge was to protect himself. First.

He remembered the empty plastic bag in the tree-guard box. "Clumsier than rubber gloves but it'll do the trick."

He couldn't hear his own voice over Butch's yowling.

Slipping the bag over his hand, he caught his breath and shoved his rolled-up, burger-sized T-shirt against Butch's wound. Hard.

The action got the child's attention.

"What — ?" he cried.

Davey cut him off, gentled him. "Look, Butch, I know all this blood is scary. But you've got lots more inside, I promise." *I hope.*

Butch did a slow thoughtful nod. His eyes and nose kept running. *Good kid*, thought Davey.

Now what? he wondered, his mind racing through choices. *Should I run for the house? Activate the*

Emergency Medical Services system? Get help?

But the house was a quarter mile away.

By the time I could get to a phone, Davey decided, *his heart'll have pumped out most of little Butch's blood — he's only got about a half-gallon milk jug's worth. No, if Butch is gonna live, I have to stop the bleed here, now. Before I do anything else.*

As quickly as thoughts rushed through his mind, he made plans.

Once the blood starts to clot and the bleed is under control, I'll move him.

First things first.

* * *

"I want you to please lie down. No questions. Just do it." Davey's voice was soft and firm. "Please!"

Butch did it.

Davey lifted Butch's arm, pad and all. With Butch's injured wrist in the air above his chest, his heart needed to pump blood uphill for it to escape from the wound. It was a simple way to slow the flow.

Davey hoped.

From underneath Davey's plastic-bagged hand, blood continued to curl down and across Butch's forearm. It was pouring off his funny bone.

Butch's eyes went up his elevated limb. The folded T-shirt, held against the puncture, was more red than white.

The grass was splattered with blood.

Butch was biting his bottom lip. Davey thought, *I'd probably be screaming my head off.*

The T-shirt was saturated.

Is it any better? Are clots forming? Davey knew he shouldn't lift the pad to check. He didn't want to disturb the natural blood-stopping mechanism. But, from what he could see, pressure and elevation didn't seem to be working.

"I need your help, Butch. Here, you hold down the T-shirt." He grabbed Butch's left hand and placed it over the wound. "Tight."

Butch followed directions. He looked less scared as soon as he had something to do.

Davey pulled his folded bandanna out of his back pocket. Then slipped it under Butch's hand, on top of the shirt.

Butch was doing a good job holding direct pressure. A second dressing — the bandanna — had been added to soak up any new flow.

Davey knew that, if direct pressure didn't work, Butch wasn't holding the right spot. Davey tried to picture just where the puncture was. He moved Butch's hand a tad further down his injured wrist.

"Press it hard, right there," he reminded Butch.

One last thing to try . . .

Pressure point.

Davey encircled Butch's upper arm with thumb on the outside and four fingers lined up on the inside, and he felt the pulse between the bicep muscle and the upper arm-bone.

Davey squeezed his fingers right down to that bone.

There, his smile was grim, *I've got the artery that runs down his arm to his wrist.*

Mash it flat.

Davey imagined a garden hose with a hole poked in it. If you step on the hose above the leak, not so much water will come out.

If I do the pressure point right, blood won't get through this artery.

"Can I let go now?" Butch asked.

Parts of the bandanna had stayed dry. Progress.

"No. Not yet. Here's why. . . ."

* * *

Davey explained clotting to Butch so he'd keep the T-shirt and bandanna against his wrist. Then — never easing off the pressure point — Davey hefted Butch like a bushel of apples and headed for the house.

In fifteen minutes, the two were on the sofa next to the phone in the Andersons' farmhouse.

Butch sprawled over Davey's lap.

Davey had never let up the direct pressure on Butch's elevated upper arm.

Butch's hand clamped down the T-shirt with the bandanna on top. "Davey, won't Aunt Lydia kill me if I get blood on the sofa? Shouldn't I sit on the floor? Can I have a glass of chocolate milk?"

Davey laughed as he picked up the phone. He couldn't help it.

He needed to activate the 9-1-1 Emergency Medical Services system. A sticker on the phone listed a seven-digit emergency number: 555-5656.

"Sheriff's Department."

Davey explained the situation. "How long will it take for EMS to respond?" he said.

"When's the ambulance going to arrive? How many people will be in it?" Butch was at it again. "Will we go fast? Will the siren be loud?

"Will you be with me in the ambulance? . . . Cross your heart?"

* * *

The first responder was Leon, a Hope electrician everyone knew as Leon Neon.

Leon Neon was a volunteer emergency medical technician.

He'd been working on a job down the road when Hope's distinctive tone blared through the beeper on his belt. He drove straight to the scene, in his neon-green-and-yellow electrician's van with the twirling red light.

The muscular EMT was taking Butch's blood pressure — which was a tad low — as the ambulance pulled up outside. "Far out," Leon Neon told Davey and Butch. "Like you two got this bleed under control. But, hey, I'm not gonna mess with your dressings to confirm, ya know? Like, we'll do that in the emergency department, so if it isn't cool, the doc'll deal with it under optimum conditions. Dig?"

Davey dug. Butch dug.

Once Butch and Davey were loaded into the rig, Leon Neon announced, "We are Ten-08 for the hospital. Let's rock 'n' roll. We are outta here."

Butch liked Leon Neon.

As the ambulance backed out of the Andersons' driveway, Leon Neon turned to Butch. "Okay kid, I'd like you to breathe in some heavy-duty O's through this oxygen mask. Your body's gonna be so happy to see 'em comin'. . . ."

* * *

On a glorious day like this, it was tough for Davey to imagine that, seven days before, Butch had almost bled out in this same orchard.

Davey had thought he wouldn't want to see an apple tree again but, when Butch's family asked him to a picnic on the last afternoon of their vacation in Maine, it sounded like fun.

He'd always liked the Andersons, and sure felt he had a connection with their nephew and his parents.

While they all lazed in the sun, Butch, his wrist bandaged, hung out near Davey. The adults and Davey were reliving that afternoon the week before.

The two Anderson couples had had a fun afternoon aboard the lobster boat *Betselma*.

Davey and Butch had had their own excitement.

As the last piece of apple cobbler disappeared, Mr. Anderson nudged Butch.

Butch moved toward Davey, extending a gift-wrapped box.

Everyone was beaming as Davey unwrapped it."Oh wow. WOW." He turned the Red Sox hat in his hands, feeling its fabric and eyeing its faded red color.

Butch's father said, "My brother here told us how you lost your cap last winter. I've worn this one since sixty-seven when my dad bought it for me at Fenway. Last game of the season. Red Sox and Twins. You know about the Impossible Dream season?"

Butch took the red hat with the blue-black bill out of Davey's hands and put it on his head, visor in the back. "This is because," Butch wore a grown-up expression as he adjusted the hat on Davey's head, "we're blood brothers."

"Forever," answered Davey, high-fiving him. On Butch's good arm.

Controlling Hemorrhage

WHAT is it? Stopping spurting blood.

WHY do you do it? If you don't, the bleeding can kill within three minutes. Applying pressure pinches the damaged artery, slows blood flow, and buys time for clots to form.

WHEN do you do it? Whenever there is bleeding.

HOW do you do it? 1) Put something — paper towels, gauze pads, cloth (the cleaner the better) — on the wound to absorb blood. 2) Place a protected hand on the cloth or pad and press hard. 3) Unless there might be broken bones, raise the bleeding area above the level of the heart. 4) Don't ease the pressure until a medical professional tells you to. Don't peek at it. 5) If blood soaks through, add more T-shirt or diaper or gauze or whatever on top of what is already there. 6) If nothing is working and there is a pressure point between the bleed and the heart, use a second hand to compress the artery against the bone.

Is the scene safe?

Before helping save someone else's life, make sure the scene is safe — for you. Touching anyone else's blood is not safe.

Four places where the human body has pressure points. These are the spots where an artery is between a bone and the skin surface.

To protect yourself from disease, *you must place something* — rubber gloves, Saran Wrap, a plastic bag, a thick cloth — *between yourself and others' blood.* Rubber gloves are best.

If you can, teach the bleeding person how to control the bleed. Use his or her hands, rather than yours.

Wash your hands after. Ask a medical professional for special disinfectant soap.

Do not touch your mouth, eyes, or nose before you've had a chance to wash.

* * *

To learn more about controlling bleeding, read *American Red Cross First Aid: Responding to Emergencies*, published by Mosby Year Book, 1991.

Emergency Rescue! Report

Report number 9	My name *Davey Mountain*

Incident location
Hope Orchard
street
Hope , Maine
city/town   state

My address
Sea Street
street
Camden, ME 04843
city/town   state   zip

Was the scene safe? yes ☒ no ☒ → *I had to protect myself from blood.*
Describe the scene.
I was doing a good job babysitting. It was just an accident.

First name of victim *Butch*	Age 6	male ☒	female ☐	**Aid first given by** ☒ me ☐ someone else ☐ EMTs ☐ police ☐ firefighters

Transported to *Penboscot Bay Hospital*

Describe any transportation or communication problems. *We were a quarter-mile from a phone.*

Type of illness or injury or accident
☐ bone fracture
☐ aches and sprains
☒ bleeding injury   *artery !!!*
☐ illness
☐ fire
☐ auto or truck accident
☐ water incident
☐ HazMat
☐ airplane disaster
☐ lost person/search and rescue
☐ extrication
☐ animal incident
☐ electrical accident
☐ tornado
☐ hurricane
☐ blizzard
☐ other

Who called for help?
☒ me
☐ a friend
☐ family member
☐ professional responder
☐ neighbor
☐ other person

Emergency responders on the scene
☒ EMTs
☐ firefighters
☐ police
☐ HazMat
☐ emergency department
☐ utility crew
☐ search and rescue

Describe what happened, and the outcome. Include unusual circumstances. *Butch punctured an artery. He and I controlled it finally. Then I carried him to a phone. Leon Neon took over.*

my signature *Davey Mountain*

5
Clue

"Matt. Matt. MATT!!!!" A hasty team of three trained searchers, sent ahead of other rescuers, was sweeping the area.

Paramedic Jim Morris, Matt's English teacher, was at the lead. "MAAAAT. Ho, MAAAT. Can you hear me?"

Was Matt dreaming?

He opened an eye, couldn't figure out where he was.

Then he remembered the Windjammer Outing Club's annual camping experience here in northern Maine. It was Matt's first trip as a junior member.

And here he was, in the middle of the night, lost. But maybe just found?

"Here I am! HELLLLPPPP. Hey, I'm heeeeeere! Me, Matt!"

Then they were there with him, their headlamps playing all over him like beacons of protection. "Howya doin', Matt?" Asking how he felt, if he was hurt.

Someone placed a down jacket over his shoulders.

He felt perfect. Great. Like crawling under the covers on a cold winter evening and pulling them up over your head. Relaxing your body as the warmth sweeps over.

Matt would never again feel so . . . *found*.

And stupid, of course. He felt dumb.

"I guess," he said, looking down at the insulated coat bundled around his hands, "Todd must be some mad. Not that I blame him."

Matt and Todd got turned around the day before when Todd took off for the base camp alone. Matt refused to move. He was going to do what you're supposed to do when you're lost. Don't wander. Blow a whistle. Find a space. Show your face. That's the ticket.

And look what it got him — an evening out in the wild with the bugs. Todd probably back at camp with the other guys, gloating, while adults had to spend the night out searching for him. . . .

"Todd?" Paramedic Jim Morris straightened. "Where *is* Todd? Not here?" He looked up at the other two hasty team members.

John held the radio to his mouth: "Portable-9. Search and Rescue Command," he said to the warden at the other end. "Advise you request permission to upgrade to SAR Level Two. . . ."

He pronounced the acronym for search and rescue, SAR, so it rhymed with jar.

". . . We've located one, but the other kid is still Ten-60 and" — glancing at the lowering clouds and fog — "the Ten-13's deteriorating."

* * *

By 0500 the next morning, as the sun rose behind the mountains, Todd had been overdue for a day and a half.

When Matt had been found, Mr. and Mrs. Zito, the outing club sponsors, became optimistic. They hoped Todd would show up, too, perhaps even under his own steam.

Three hasty teams made up of Outing Club members with maps and compasses searched through the night and through the following day.

Still no Todd.

The Zitos and the district warden agreed it was time for SAR Level Three.

Statewide, the Maine Warden Service geared up for a full-blown search and rescue operation.

Matt watched as one green truck after another —

the Maine Warden Service's SAR overhead team —
rolled into camp. The team's job was to organize and
manage the SAR function.

While team members moved about setting up a
communications center, supply truck, kitchen, and
sleeping accommodations, their incident commander Lt. Lightfoot debriefed Matt in the Zito tent
that now had an official sign out front:

OVERHEAD TEAM HEADQUARTERS

Inside, the lieutenant was sitting across a camp
table from Matt, her thick chestnut-colored braid
over one shoulder. LT. ANN LIGHTFOOT read her silver
name tag. There were shoulder patches on her
pressed uniform. A neat emblem over her pocket
identified her as a technical rescue climber. "What
we'll all be searching for," her voice reminded Matt
of his mom's, "is not Todd. . . ."

"You won't," Matt's face scrunched, "search for
Todd? How come?"

The warden smiled. Now she made him think of
his grown sister Stacy Rich. "Search is a mystery.
We look for clues. Todd, of course, is the ultimate
clue."

Matt knew something about SAR missions.

Aunt Jill and Uncle David Mountain were members of a SAR group. So was Stacy, a wilderness
first responder who gave remote medical help

within the seventeen million acres of Maine's woods.

Matt and Davey loved to listen to stories when they all returned home, sometimes after several days out in the field.

This was different. For the first time Matt discovered that search is a matter of life and death.

Todd's.

Matt rubbed his bum leg — the one he'd injured a couple of years ago when he and a tree collided — as he watched the incident commander straighten the bottom edges of an eight-page Lost Person Questionnaire against the metal tabletop.

"You were the last person with Todd," said Lt. Lightfoot, passing him the neat sheaf of papers. "You might not realize it, but you have information no one else does. We need to know where Todd is, mentally, to find him physically."

"We need to know," her gray eyes bored into Matt's blue ones, "*everything* you know."

He shoved his blond hair off his forehead, angled the form, and picked up the pencil with the square fingers of his left hand.

The weight was on Matt's shoulders, like the time his dog Chancealong's mother stopped breathing and he had to save her. He tried to put the pressure aside, and remember what had happened right before Todd took off.

*   *   *

LOST PERSON DATA

name ___TODD BULLOCK_____ age _17___ sex _MALE_
nickname _SOME CALL HIM BULL BUT NOT TO HIS FACE.___

PHYSICAL DESCRIPTION

hair: color _BROWN____ length _MEDIUM____ style _?___
face: shape _EGG_____ complexion _TAN, PIMPLES ON CHIN_
photo available? _MARCIE HAS ONE IN HER WALLET._
build _LARGE_____ height _6 FEET____ weight _ABOUT 185_

CLOTHING

shirt _BLUE+RED PLAID COTTON_ rainwear _NO_____
pants _BAGGY_____ hat _RED___ footwear _BOOTS, HUGE!_
Subject's overall coloration as seen from air? _RED_____

EQUIPMENT

matches _NO____ compass _NO___ map _NO___ knife _DON'T THINK
food _NO, MAYBE SOME ATOMIC FIRE BALLS_____ SO

TRIP PLANS

WE WERE JUST GOING OUT FOR A HALF HOUR. WE WEREN'T
PLANNING ON GETTING LOST.

HABITS

smoker _NO____ gum/candy/etc. _LIKES ATOMIC FIRE BALL CANDIES_

HEALTH

physical condition _A LITTLE FLAB, NOT MUCH_____
medications _?_____
eyesight _WEARS GLASSES TO DRIVE_ glasses _I DIDN'T SEE THEM._

PERSONALITY

fears _HE'S AFRAID OF LOOKING LIKE A SISSY._
feelings toward adults _OKAY_
feelings toward strangers _TALKS, GETS FRIENDLY_
reaction when hurt/sick _TRIES TO HIDE IT BUT I SAW HIM CRY ONCE_
Will he/she admit being wrong? _NO WAY_   WHEN HE
fictional hero _ANY TOM CRUISE CHARACTER_   TWISTED HIS
Gives up easily?/Presses on? _MAYBE HE GIVES UP, BUT HE_   ANKLE.
                    DOESN'T LET ANYONE KNOW.

"Phew." Matt let go of his pencil after he'd completed the first four pages. He flexed his cramped fingers on an imaginary tennis ball — so much writing was wrecking his hand.

* * *

Todd was a basket case.

It was now a day and a half that he'd been lost.

His clothes were torn and dirty. His knees were scraped. Face, neck, and forearm were covered with welts, scratched raw.

Todd felt hungry, frightened, and abandoned.

His shouted conversation with a non-existent Matt — "You can't fool me, Matt!" — was crazed. "I know you're right behind that tree. Stop hiding!"

For the first six hours after he had left Matt, Todd had a plan. He'd aimed to get to the top of a ridge where he could look out and find something familiar. Then run back and get Matt, as he had promised.

But every ridge he climbed seemed to lead higher. There was always in the distance another spot, offering a better view.

His spirits sank with dusk. Fog didn't help.

Losing his sight had always been Todd's greatest fear. He never played games like Blind Man's Buff or Marco Polo. Now he was trapped within the pitch-black darkness of the Maine woods.

When the rain rolled in from the west at dawn the next morning, Todd was caught unprepared.

Since then, he had walked in cold, wet clothes.

"I see you, Matt. Hah!" he yelled at a shadow deep in the gloom.

Todd was physically and emotionally whipped.

As the evening of the second day rolled around, once again the weather was going down the tubes.

Todd wasn't far behind.

The first stab of lightning hit the top of a huge white pine several hundred yards to Todd's left. With a flash and a deafening roar, the top half of the tree trunk split in two.

The force threw Todd to the ground. He lay there, eyes shut and arms thrown over his head.

He heard screaming. *Who was that?* It took him a moment to realize that it was him.

That's when it started to rain. Hard.

The next morning was overcast. No sunshine to dry out the woods. Todd's street pants and shirt clung to his body, offering no warmth.

In between the times when he acted as if a sea gull had flown into his hair, he did have moments of sanity. But they didn't help him figure out where he was or where he was going. All he could think about was how the camp had to be around the next ridge. *No? Well, maybe over there, across the brook and beyond that . . .*

As a small beam of sun crossed his path, he removed his red hat. He turned his face toward the ray of warmth.

The hat slipped from his fingers.

Todd bent over and picked up his hat. In the last thirty-six hours it had fallen off dozens of times, snagged on stray fir branches, blown by the wind, brushed off when Todd stooped to drink at a stream.

With a sudden viciousness, Todd threw his hat to the ground and jumped on it. His big work boots, caked with mud, drove it into the soft ground at the side of the stream.

As Matt, a pencil in his tired hand, completed the CLOTHING section of the questionnaire, Todd was yelling at his hat, *"That's the last time I'll have to deal with you! . . ."*

Matt filled in the space after *"hat"*: RED.

* * *

While Todd's hat lay sopping up moisture at the stream's edge, Lt. Lightfoot studied a topographic map which showed the ridges, valleys, mountains, and streams of the wilderness area. Sitting across the table, Matt watched her write PLS to the left of center on the unfolded topo chart.

"This is the place last seen, Matt. Where the hasty team found you. And where you — anyone — last saw Todd.

"Until we find another clue, this is our search starting point."

Then Matt watched her measure a circle around the PLS — an imaginary fence with a radius of five miles. "We know from experience," she tapped the chart with her nail, "that a typical healthy seventeen-year-old like Todd wouldn't have walked through the terrain further than here. That's an outer limit, mind you."

Within two hours, she would have lookouts in place along the mountain tops, making sure Todd did not slip through the circle she just drew on her map.

Limit the world, Matt rationalized, where Todd can be. Then search inside it.

The first step had been taken.

It made sense to Lt. Lightfoot.

And to Matt.

The lieutenant turned to say something to him. "Now, I have the unpleasant duty of — " The racket of a helicopter blasted her words away. In addition to lookouts peering through binoculars in search of a red-hatted individual, a chopper would be scanning the containment area for Todd.

Lt. Lightfoot's mouth was grim as she picked up her radio. "Patch me through to his parents now, Ten-03?"

With dust and leaves swirling outside the tent, the chopper took off.

The tent walls flapped. Matt's pencil rolled off the camp table with the chatter. His canvas seat felt like a vibrating chair.

"How could Todd ever miss *that*?" Matt wore his hopeful expression.

*   *   *

The helicopter hovered. Todd was sure the deafening noise overhead was another thunderstorm.

As he dove for cover, his chest whomped against the ground. His last Fire Ball projected out of his mouth with the impact, and dropped at the base of a beech tree.

Todd clung to the trunk.

The thunder rolled nearer, washed over him.

It paralyzed him. He never looked up to see the green-and-white belly of the helicopter streak overhead.

As soon as it was safe, Todd bolted to the northwest.

He didn't know that 250 feet away, a clue-conscious searcher was being berated by an angry camper. ". . . And you're telling me we have to fold up our tent and move on?" The man's jowled face was red as his voice rose over the chopper's noise. "Hey, the wife and I drove ten hours from Newark, New Jersey, just to camp and fish this spot. We've got a camping permit. We take care of the woods. We pick up others' litter — cigarette butts, cans, candy wrappers, things like that — and pack it out. Why should we have to leave?"

The containment circle was being tightened as trained personnel entered the field, sweeping the area for people who would confuse the search.

Sportsmen, climbers, berry pickers — all had to be removed to keep the trail fresh and clues in place.

So two unhappy New Jersey campers hiked back three miles to their car. They threw a plastic bag of garbage into the trunk, put their vehicle in gear, and burned rubber as a departing statement.

*　*　*

As the Newark couple drove away with their bag of trash containing one of Todd's Fire Ball wrappers, a waist-high string was being strung from tree to tree. In the woods, Lt. Lightfoot's imaginary fence on the topo map was turned into the actual perimeter of the search area.

A four-man team — Matt, Marcie, and two other Outing Club members — was navigating the correct line, spooling out string from a backpack, and tying it to trees.

Matt hung blaze-orange cardboard arrows pointing toward the camp.

All Todd had to do was to follow the arrows and he'd end up at SAR headquarters.

Matt paused, staring at the arrow in his hand.

"Hey, Matt, cheer up." Marcie broke into his thoughts. "We'll get him." She patted Matt on his back, turned to start spooling.

Matt noted that Marcie was no longer wearing her

Support
Search and Rescue
— get lost!

T-shirt. What a joke.

It was now 1800 of the third day. Another dinner time that Todd would be missing.

When did you start to worry about starvation?
Now.

Matt, his head down, hiked back along the stream toward camp with Marcie.

Something caught his eye.

It was red.

It was wet and dirty.

He bent and picked it up, trying not to hope too much.

"Hey hey hey!!! Todd's hat!"

The helicopter was radioed to stop looking for a red-hatted person.

The discovery of the hat added more data on where Todd had been, and the direction of travel. Although the Atomic Fire Ball cellophane had ended up on its way to Newark, the candy Todd had spit out was found at the foot of the beech tree.

One of these clues had to be the LKP, the last known place where Todd had been.

As soon as Matt was back at the command center, he dropped the pile of blaze-orange arrows and headed for the topo map.

Someone had plotted, not far from Lt. Lightfoot's PLS, the location of the half-sucked Atomic Fire Ball.

Matt picked up a pencil and marked the map where he had found Todd's red hat. The three points were in almost a straight line.

They pointed to the northwest, away from the PLS and the Outing Club campsite.

Now, thought Matt, *if he keeps moving in this direction and he's still in the containment area, he's bound to run into our string line.*

* * *

Todd was first aware of the string line only when he walked into it.

He came out of his daze enough to realize what it was.

He screamed for joy.

"Matt! Matt!" He turned and started running. "I know which way to go, Matt. I'm coming to get you, like I promised."

He began to move in a new direction, the southeast. Whether it was luck or some primeval instinct, Todd headed for the PLS, where he had last seen Matt.

* * *

Janey Waterpaws was pumped. She was sniffing, then she sat down. She jumped up again and started to whimper. She turned toward the direction of a new voice.

Matt gave her a Milk-Bone. She licked his hand, then daintily took the treat.

"Go for it, Janey," Matt urged her. Janey Waterpaws was his last hope.

Janey, the bloodhound, had been flown in with her handlers.

Now the man-tracking dog was presented with a shirt from Todd's pack. This scent item contained millions of Todd's sluffed-off body cells.

Those same cells would leave a wide but invisible

trail wherever Todd had traveled. Janey could sniff it out.

Janey Waterpaws was taken to the LKP, Todd's last known point, where Matt had discovered his red hat.

From there, Janey would track Todd in the dark, nose-to-ground.

The dog was the boss, stopping when she wished, running as she wanted.

Her handlers trailed behind.

It looked like a pretty silly setup to Matt. He was waiting for a dumb dog to find Todd in the dark of night.

Stacy was driving up from Camden to offer medical support to the SAR effort. But he, Matt, had nothing to do but sit.

And worry.

Actually he needed some support from Stacy as well. Moral support.

He was giving up. And fed up.

Where was Todd?

Matt couldn't stand to think about it anymore.

He knew it wasn't his fault. He felt it was all his fault.

He wanted to escape.

Sighing, he flipped the pages of a book Lt. Lightfoot had suggested he read. *Inferno* was about survival sense — the ability some kids show when they're in death-defying situations.

After a half hour of reading, he closed the book and considered its message.

What can I do, Matt wondered, *when all that's being done isn't working? I've got to think differently than the adults out there. I've got to think like a kid, like Todd.*

What would Todd do? Matt pondered.

He held his head in his hands, his elbows propped on his knees. As he sat there shaking his head, Todd's last words came back: *"Hey, you want to sit here — fine. Fine. I'll start back, and when I see something you'll remember, I'll come back and get you."*

". . . I'll come back and. . . ."

He heard the sound of a VW bus.

Matt looked out the tent flap and saw Stacy pull in and park between a couple of Warden Service trucks.

"Stacy!" he called to her as she slammed the VW's door. "I've got a hunch. . . ."

* * *

". . . And there he was, filthy dirty, weak, skinny, leaning against a stump right in the middle of the PLS." An hour after her arrival, Stacy was talking to a beaming Lt. Lightfoot. "And he had the *gall* to walk up to Matt and go, 'There you are, where've you been? I been looking all over for you. Ready to be led back to the camp?' "

Go ahead and laugh, thought Matt, *all of you*, as he watched everyone crack up. *Ha ha.*

He wanted to kill Todd.

And hug him. The greatest moment of his life had been when he radioed: "Portable-M, SAR Command.

We're Ten-19 with the ultimate clue, the Ten-60."

And he had to smile at the way Janey Waterpaws, her handlers stretched out behind her, had come bounding up to Todd about fifteen seconds after Stacy and Matt found him.

The dog just sat drooling over Todd, expecting her reward. It seemed that praise for Janey was throwing a stick for her, over and over. Right away.

As Stacy checked out Todd medically, Matt tossed a hunk of wood for the dog.

When Janey brought it back to him for the tenth time, he noticed some words stitched on her nylon collar. He pulled her close and read:

IF YOU DON'T CARE WHERE YOU ARE, THEN YOU AIN'T LOST.

SKILL
Defining the Search Area

WHAT is it? Planning and taking steps so that, when someone or something is lost, you know where it isn't — which is the way to find something.

WHY do you do it? So you will find the lost person or thing efficiently.

WHEN do you do it? Whenever anything is lost — your dad's car keys or your pal. For the best chance at success, and so that clues are preserved, go to work as soon as possible after the loss.

HOW do you do it? 1) Gather information about where, when, and how the loss happened. 2) Eliminate areas where you are sure the thing is not. 3) Know how far it could have traveled. Then draw a perimeter circle on paper or in your mind that the searched-for object has to be within. Do this carefully, because, if it turns out that the item is not in your containment area, then it could be anywhere in the world. 4) Close off your search area to make sure the lost object doesn't walk through, or get carried out of the containment area. If someone is disturbing things in the confinement area without preserving clues, that person, like the New Jersey campers, should be asked to leave. 5) Within the containment area, first survey the PLS. Then, as clues develop, check out any LKPs. Search least likely places last. 6) Put yourself into the mind of the person who is lost, or who misplaced the item, like Matt did. Recreate in your imagination what they were thinking and doing. 7) Be logical. Think through all possibilities. 8) Consider what you can do when everything everyone is doing isn't working.

Is the scene safe?

When you are defining a containment area, then searching, always be certain to know where *you* are.

* * *

To learn more about containment areas, read *Wilderness Search and Rescue* by Tim J. Setnicka, published by Appalachian Mountain Club, 1980.

Emergency Rescue! Report

Report number 10	My name MATT RICH

Incident location

TOWN 7, RANGE 10 - WOODS
street UNORGANIZED
TERRITORY OF MAINE
city/town   state

My address

BAY VIEW STREET
street
CAMDEN, ME. 04843
city/town   state   zip

Was the scene safe? yes ☒ no ☐ AS LONG AS I TAKE
~~Describe the scene.~~
ALONG MY FANNY PACK WITH MY MATCHES,
COMPASS, BUG DOPE, AND OTHER EMERGENCY STUFF. YOU NEVER
KNOW WHEN YOU MIGHT GET LOST!

First name of victim TODD	Age 17	male ☒	female ☐	Aid first given by

Aid first given by
☒ me
☒ someone else
☐ EMTs WFR
☐ police STACY
☐ firefighters

Transported to MILLINOCKET HOSPITAL

Describe any transportation WE WERE IN THE
or communication problems. MIDDLE OF
THE GREAT NORTH WOODS

Type of illness or injury or accident
☐ bone fracture
☐ aches and sprains
☐ bleeding injury
☐ illness
☐ fire
☐ auto or truck accident
☐ water incident
☐ HazMat
☐ airplane disaster
☒ lost person/search and rescue
☐ extrication
☐ animal incident
☐ electrical accident
☐ tornado
☐ hurricane
☐ blizzard
☐ other

Who called for help?
☐ me
☐ a friend
☐ family member
☐ professional responder
☐ neighbor
☒ other person THE ZITOS

Emergency responders on the scene
☐ EMTs
☐ firefighters
☐ police
☐ HazMat
☐ emergency department
☐ utility crew
☒ search and rescue

Describe what happened, and the outcome. Include unusual circumstances. WHEN TODD AND ME GOT SEPARATED,
HE KEPT MOVING. THE FOREST IS SO HUGE, IT
TOOK A WHOLE LOT OF PEOPLE 3 DAYS TO
FIND HIM.

my signature *Matt Rich*

Emergency Rescue!
Vocabulary

adrenaline: this chemical, made by the body and released when you get excited, also reverses allergic reactions

altered mental state: acting and talking differently than usual

artery: oxygen-rich blood flows away from the heart through these hollow tubes

arterial bleed: a dire emergency when lots of blood pumps out of the body

beeper: a radio receiver, the size of a stack of baseball cards, that lets rescuers know when they are needed

blood pressure: the force of the pumping heart as it squeezes blood throughout the body

blood vessels: veins and arteries that deliver blood

body heat: warmth created when food-fuel burns

certified lifesaver: a person trained and tested in water rescue

charley horse: a nickname for a cramp

clot: a soft clump of blood that corks bleeding wounds

cold challenge: an attack by wind, temperature, and moisture that drains body heat

cold reduction: limiting the challenge of cold

coma: a state of unconsciousness one cannot be awakened from

compress: to press against with or without a pad; to squeeze together

containment area: where a lost person is and will stay until found

core: the central, most important parts of the human body

cramp: a painful muscle tightening

critical: life-threatening

dire emergency: a situation that will result in death unless changed

direct pressure: the force of a gloved hand on a wound to help clotting and control bleeding

disinfectant: a germ killer

dispatcher: answers emergency calls, sends responders, then coaches callers until rescuers are on the scene

dressing: a pad protecting a wound

drownproofing: a lifesaving method to float, breathe, and conserve your energy when in trouble in the water

electrical shock: the feeling of current passing through the body

electrocution: death caused by a strong electrical shock

elevate: in medical terms, to lift above the heart

EMS: stands for Emergency Medical Services, the network of medical responders — from citizen responders, like you, to dispatchers, EMTs, and finally hospital emergency department doctors and nurses

EMT: Emergency Medical Technician, a professional responder who treats patients at the scene and in the ambulance on the way to the hospital

energized: charged and tingling with electricity

extremities: arms and legs

first responder: the emergency rescuer first at the scene

fog pattern: a fire hose's wide, superfine water spray

hasty team: the first-responding search and rescue team, a few trained joggers who look quickly in the most-likely areas for an overdue person

heat production: creating warmth

heat reduction: the removal of heat

heat retention: conserving warmth

hemorrhage: loss of a large amount of blood in a short period of time

hot (or live) wire: charged with electricity

hyperventilate: to breathe rapidly

hypothermia, mild: a below-normal core temperature, as the body loses its battle to keep warm

hypothermia, severe: a very low core temperature, less than 90° F (normal is 98.6°F)

incident commander: SAR mission boss

insulate: to surround with material that slows the flow of heat or electricity

LKP: the last known point where the object of a search was

line crew: the electric company's emergency responders

muscle contraction: a tightening or shortening of muscle fibers

muscle fiber: fine, threadlike body tissue drawn together like rope

on call: available and ready to respond to an emergency

overdue: rescue term for later than expected, perhaps lost

overhead team: a statewide management group trained to run search and rescue operations

PD: short for police department

paralysis: inability to feel and move a portion of the body

paramedic: a person with the highest EMT certification

PFD: personal flotation device, such as a life jacket

PLS: SAR language for the place a lost person was last seen

portable-: short for **portable** radio, and also used to identify a rescuer through his portable number; Davey and Matt call themselves **Portable**-D and **Portable**-M

pressure point: where you can squeeze an artery against a bone (see *pulse*)

primary survey: a quick body check for life-threatening emergencies

pulse: this beat of the pumping heart can be felt wherever an artery stretches over a bone — at the wrist, on the top of the feet, along the neck, and in the groin (see *pressure point*)

puncture wound: a penetrating cut through skin and tissue made by an object

remote: more than one hour away from a hospital

rig: nickname for an ambulance

rock 'n' roll: EMT slang for packaging and transporting to a hospital f-a-s-t

reach → throw → row → go: water-rescue steps, from safest to most dangerous

run: an emergency response, starting when rescuers are called and ending when they and their rig are back in the station

SAR: stands for search and rescue, an organized attempt to find an overdue person

secondary survey: head-to-toe medical check

shock: when blood stops delivering enough oxygen throughout the body, this dire emergency results

shunt: to take blood away from where it is least needed and send it to where it is most needed

signs: medical clues the EMT observes (see *symptoms*)

simple sugars: fast-burning fuel the body uses quickly, like Devil Dogs, Oreos, Yoo-Hoo, Life Savers

spinal cord: bundles of nerves inside the backbone

stat: immediately; hustle!

string line: lightweight containment-area fence

survival sense: the ability and strength to overcome life-threatening challenges

symptoms: the patient's complaints (see *signs*)

terrain: the rise and fall of the land

topo(graphy) map: a chart of mountains, plains, hills, and valleys along with the usual features on road maps like lakes, bridges, and highways

trauma: damage to the body; injury usually from a blow, fall, or cut

unconscious: unable to see, hear, and feel

vasoconstriction: a tightening of fluid-carrying body parts

voltage: electric current's force

warden: what forest rangers are called in the state of Maine

wilderness first responder: a licensed first aider, like Stacy, trained in backcountry emergencies; nicknamed woofer

About the Authors

The Cowans, with eight children from 12 to 34, battle fires and respond to medical emergencies in mid-Coast Maine, join in search and rescue missions throughout the northeast, and through a federal network of medical teams, respond worldwide to earthquakes, floods, and other natural disasters. Wilderness-EMTs, American National Red Cross Instructors for the Professional Rescuer, and Maine Emergency Medical Technicians, they run with The Wilderness Rescue Team, belong to the National Association of Search and Rescue, and the National Association of EMS Physicians.

Share your emergency adventures
with the authors!

Whenever you witness an emergency, send us your filled-out Emergency Rescue! Report, on the next page. Even if you don't have an incident to report right now, we'd still love to know what you like about our *EMERGENCY RESCUE!* books. We will respond to your letter or report. Ten-04?

> The Cowans
> EMERGENCY RESCUE!
> Mountain Street
> Camden, ME 04843

Emergency Rescue! Report Instructions

1. If this book is borrowed from a library or a friend, you need to make a copy of the Emergency Rescue! Report form, on the opposite page. If this is your own book, tear or cut out the page.
2. Fill out the Emergency Rescue! Report form.
3. Then fold on the dotted line.
4. Tape or staple the unfolded bottom edges shut.
5. Place a stamp where it says to.
6. Mail it.

Emergency Rescue! Report

Report number	My name

Incident location	My address

_____ | _____
street | street

_____ | _____
city/town   state | city/town   state   zip

Was the scene safe? yes no
Describe the scene. ☐ ☐

First name of victim	Age	male ☐	female ☐	Aid first given by

Transported to

☐ me
☐ someone else
☐ EMTs
☐ police
☐ firefighters

Describe any transportation
or communication problems.

Type of illness or injury or accident

☐ bone fracture
☐ aches and sprains
☐ bleeding injury
☐ illness
☐ fire
☐ auto or truck accident
☐ water incident
☐ HazMat
☐ airplane disaster
☐ lost person/search and rescue
☐ extrication
☐ animal incident
☐ electrical accident
☐ tornado
☐ hurricane
☐ blizzard
☐ other

Who called for help?

☐ me
☐ a friend
☐ family member
☐ professional
   responder
☐ neighbor
☐ other person

Emergency responders on the scene

☐ EMTs
☐ firefighters
☐ police
☐ HazMat
☐ emergency department
☐ utility crew
☐ search and rescue

Describe what happened, and the outcome. Include unusual
circumstances.

my signature _____

Staple or tape shut . . . stamp . . . and mail.

Plac
stan
here

Emergency Rescue!
Mountain Street
Camden, Maine 04843